BROKEN DOLL

NEIL CAMPBELL was born in Audenshaw, Manchester in 1973. While working variously as a warehouseman, bookseller and teacher, he had poems and stories published in small press magazines, and now edits *Lamport Court*. In 1999, at Manchester University, he completed an MA dissertation on the short stories of Raymond Carver, and in 2006 graduated, with a distinction, from the Creative Writing MA at Manchester Metropolitan University. This is his first book.

NEIL CAMPBELL

Broken Doll

SALT

CAMBRIDGE

PUBLISHED BY SALT PUBLISHING
PO Box 937, Great Wilbraham, Cambridge PDO CB21 5JX United Kingdom

Salt Publishing 2007

Printed and bound in the United Kingdom by Lightning Source
Typeset in Swift 9.5 / 13

ISBN-13 978 1 84471 301 1 paperback

Salt Publishing Ltd gratefully acknowledges
the financial assistance of Arts Council England

1 3 5 7 9 8 6 4 2

For my parents, and my sister

Contents

THE ORANGE FOOTBALL

From the bridge, Phil could see their orange ball bouncing around in the dusk and he ran onto the fields to join them. Richard was between the trees, from which hung their jumpers and jackets, and Dave immediately chipped the ball over for Phil. The game was goomer and the idea was to score with either a header or a volley, but, having just turned up, Phil was out of practice and volleyed his first shot high above the trees and onto the sloping embankment beside the railway line. Ignoring their groans, he sprinted after the ball and climbed the silver wire fence that gave with his weight like the loose ropes of a boxing ring. Retrieving the ball from within the scraping eaves of a blackberry bush, he paused to grab some berries before climbing back up the slope and hurling the ball back over the fence, where it bounced on the blackening grass and rolled towards Richard and Dave beside the goal trees.

As the darkness slowed in on the humid summer night, they continued to kick the orange ball between them and, squinting in readiness for a header, Phil felt the mud stick on his forehead and heard the ball bounce off the post. With sweaty feet and head itching from the mud, Phil moaned that he couldn't see, so they stopped and sat on the grass and had no energy to get up and throw stones at the train that sent light passing over them, like speeded-up footage of the day.

Lying on his back, Phil felt the grass tickle his ears, and then the ball rebounding from his head.

'Get up you lazy bastard,' said Dave.

'Get lost! What did you do that for?' said Phil.

'Come on, lads,' said Richard.

'Shut up, Dick,' said Dave.

'Yeah, shut up,' said Phil.

'Hey, look, she's there,' said Dave, pointing over the railway line towards Gillian Madeley, standing with her back to the window, instantly recognizable with her long black hair falling to the small of her back.

Scurrying over the field towards the silver wire fence, they climbed over and stumbled down the tough dry grass on the embankment down to the rubble of white stones bunched beneath the lines, before looking either way and darting across towards the signal tower. Climbing one by one up the metal steps, they got to the little platform behind the faintly buzzing signal box and sat huddled together on the ribbed metal base, their legs dangling above the opposite embankment that led to Gillian's garden, and their eyes peering at the white oblong of her window.

They sat there for hours until, just as they were beginning to get cold, she rushed past from right to left. She had been fully clothed, but the brevity of the glimpse made them think she was undressing. Pressed close together and wedged for safety with the barrier across their chests and under their armpits, they gazed hopefully towards the window and so failed to notice Gillian's dad in the back garden, standing with his arms folded and slowly figuring out the parts of their black blob.

After he'd shouted at them they climbed bashfully back down the metal ladder, crossed the moonlit lines and the silver wire fence and walked back across the fields, looking back after a few minutes to see Gillian closing her curtains and her father going back in through the patio door.

'She must do that on purpose,' said Richard.

'Yeah, maybe she likes it,' said Dave.

'Well, we won't be able to sit there again anyway,' said Phil.

'I don't care anyway, my arse is freezing,' said Richard.

'Shut up, Dick,' said Dave, as they passed the artificial cricket pitch and their school before reaching the street they all lived on.

In the morning the three of them walked the short distance to school. Their form room was in an old chemistry lab, and they trailed in through the open door to see that Ellis had lit one of the bunsen burners on the desk and the rest of the form had gathered around to watch as he burned Brett Mason's tie, the gassy orange igniting the bullet-holed kipper and bringing Mason's face closer and closer to the flame.

'Ellis! Stop that right now!' shouted Mr Ward, the normally genial form tutor. All the boys went back to their seats, and Mason was especially happy to be able to acknowledge the register, which he did so after tucking away the charred ends of his tie. Ellis wasn't finished yet though, and waited for Mr Ward's eyes to look back down at the register before hurling a rubber bung that bounced off the back of Mason's head and rebounded with a clatter among a rack of test tubes by the window.

After register they all trailed off to their first class of the day, Phil and Dave to Maths Group 2 and Richard to Maths Group 3. When Phil and Dave shuffled in with their bags and sat down, they were surprised to see not Mr Allcock, their regular teacher, but a supply teacher, a frizzy haired man with glasses and the beginnings of a goatee beard.

'Okay, boys, now Mr . . . your teacher says that you are to carry on with where you are up to in your exercise books. So, keep quiet,' he said, with all the authority of an ice cream.

Soon paper balls began to rain on Mr Fize. At first he said nothing about them, but when one landed in his cup and sent tea splashing over the text book he'd been pretending to read, he stood and with quivering voice said, 'Alright, you've had your fun, now keep it quiet.'

All the boys calmed down for a few minutes, but most had the instinct that they could get away with virtually anything with Mr Fize, and soon a quiet but consistent hum started to emerge from the chatter. Phil didn't join in, but Dave was among the loudest and was soon picked out by an increasingly exasperated Mr Fize.

'You! You, boy! Stop that humming. Is that clear?'

With all the class silent and watching, Dave simply nodded his head.

'I said, is that clear?'

'. . . Crystal,' said Dave, causing everyone to laugh, including Mr Fize.

The rest of the double period went by in relative peace, aside from a scream when Ellis kicked Mason, and Mr Fize, unaware that some, including Dave, had been sniffing Tipp-Ex at the back, felt he'd had them under control.

At break time, Phil and Dave met up with Richard by the rails near the grob pit.

'No Balls was off today,' said Phil.

'Oh, right. Did you have a supply teacher then?' said Richard.

'Yeah. What an idiot,' said Phil, smiling at Dave.

Behind them there was an excited chatter as someone began to descend into the grob pit. It was a school tradition to drop any spare change into it, and if anyone was prepared to run down the steps they could keep the money. The trouble was, unless they went down there when no one was around, they'd be showered with the spit of all the boys who'd rushed to the rails to watch. Some poor souls, usually new kids, didn't know the tradition, and it seemed that the lad with the spattered crew cut rushing back up the steps wouldn't easily forget his baptism.

'You alright there, Dave?'

'Yeah,' he replied, still drowsy from the correctional fluid. 'Knackered, that's all.'

'You want anything from Bolton?'

'No, I'm not hungry.'

'Alright, I'll see you at dinner then.'

Bolton was a fat lad who made what he thought were friends by doling out food from his industrial-sized lunchbox. Every morning break time he could be seen on the basketball court giving out scotch eggs, sausage rolls, bags of crisps, sticks of salted celery, buttered scones, cakes, sandwiches and chocolate bars to his fattening close circle, and yet he still had enough in the depths of his Puma bag to fill his own vast stomach. Coming away from Bolton with a thick slice of Madeira cake, Phil walked happily to the changing rooms for Games.

Phil was in the top group and one of the favourites among the Games teachers, so never had to face the indignities of those not fortunate enough to be given as much co-ordination. Once everyone had got changed they sat listening as Mr Hough told them about the upcoming trials for the cricket team. Midway through the announcement, Mason was kicked in the shins by Ellis and let out a yelp, throwing Mr Hough out of sync and annoying him to the extent that he demanded to know who'd been 'laughing'. When told that it was Mason, Mr Hough made him stand on a chair in front of the whole group.

'Right, Mason, bend over,' said Hough, twirling a spade.

'Sorry, sir?'

'I said, bend over.'

Mason duly bent over and, as he did so, Mr Hough whacked him across the backside with the spade, unintentionally hitting his coccyx and sending Mason staggering off the chair and onto the floor.

It was rugby that day and Phil managed to run in a couple of tries. Dave spent the game hanging around by the touchline. At the end of the period, as they walked with the rest of the group among the clatter of boots over the concrete leading to the changing rooms, Phil looked at his own filthy legs and then at Dave's, which were still white and un-muddied. In the showers, Phil washed himself and noticed that Dave hadn't bothered to come in with everyone else. It was a brave thing to do, risking the wrath of Mr Hough, who 'supervised' the shower area.

The following Sunday, Phil called for Richard and they both called for Dave. His mum said he was out, so Phil and Richard went over the railway bridge with their orange ball and played goomer into the empty goal between two tall trees. There was only a week left before the start of the summer holidays and there were hours and hours of daylight ahead in which to practice their headers and volleys. They had the whole oasis of the fields to themselves, save for a solitary golfer, who, with lazy swing, whacked ball after ball into the rippling distance.

Soon it was time for tea, but Phil and Richard forgot all about it, absorbed by their game. After hours and hours of goomer, they practiced bicycle kicks, one under-arming the ball for the other to jump in the air and volley. Time after time they did it, sometimes miscuing and sometimes timing their jumps perfectly to send the ball whizzing between the trees.

Phil's dad had always said that they should play football in winter and cricket in summer, so, just as the sun was starting to dip, they kicked the orange ball back and forth across the fields, intending to go home for Phil's bat, ball and wickets. Nearing the school, they ran over to move what from a distance they thought was a pile of rubbish from the artificial cricket pitch, but what they saw wasn't rubbish; it was Dave, curled in a ball, the bag of glue beside him flickering like a flower in the breeze. Phil knew he was dead because the colour of his face seemed to reflect the cloudless sky above them, and when he ran home to tell his parents, Richard sat next to Dave, too shocked to notice the smell of sick.

Soon Phil came round the corner past the school with his parents, and Richard's parents and, in front of them all, Dave's mum, squinting her eyes in the fading light and stumbling in her heels before taking them off and running barefoot across the grass. When she reached the body she began to shake it, and Phil's dad tried to pull her away as the ambulance bounced over the kerb near the school and came across the fields, headlights reaching through the dusk.

In assembly the following day, they sung a hymn as normal, before the headmaster referred to what he described as the awful news that had affected them all. He gave a lecture on the dangers of substance abuse, and only after that did he actually mention Dave by name. During the minute's silence someone farted, and a few of the boys laughed.

It was a few months before Phil and Richard went out onto the fields again, and after they'd finished playing football they walked over and sat on the artificial cricket pitch. All the flowers and tributes had gone, scattered across the fields by the wind, but as Richard sat on the orange football, making it go egg-shaped, Phil took a marker pen out of his pocket and wrote DAVE WOZ ERE across the length of the pitch, in letters so big they could have been read from the sky.

THE DISAPPEARANCE OF A SUNSET

Paul got a beer from the fridge and stood out on the balcony. A breeze rippled his shorts and the sun emerged from around the corner of the block, warming his bare white chest.

'You're up fuckin' early aren't you,' said Sarah.

'Yeah.'

'Is that the last fuckin' beer?'

'Yeah.'

'Give us some then.'

Paul looked away from Sarah's puffy red face and around at the view: the different coloured cranes, the traffic on the overpass, the procession of students, the shining glass of the Beetham Tower rising into a blue sky.

'I'm going to Blackwell's, you ready?' said Paul.

'Fuckin' hell, I've only been up a minute. Wait while I get dressed,' said Sarah.

'Fuck's sake.'

'I said I'm getting ready didn't a?'

'Well, fuckin' get on with it.'

'A fuckin' am. Dick.'

'Just fuckin' hurry up.'

When Sarah was ready she snatched the can off Paul and they walked out onto the landing. As they went down in the lift, Sarah finished the can and dropped it by her feet. In the lobby, the caretaker was mopping the floor, and when Paul and Sarah got out of the lift, they left overlapping footprints on the tiles. 'Sorry about that, love,' said Sarah.

Emerging from the cool shade at the base of the block, they walked out into the sunlight, Paul scratching the skin around his nose as Sarah playfully rubbed his crew cut.

'End of term soon, in it?' said Sarah.

'I fuckin' know, alright?'

'I'm just bleedin' sayin'' said Sarah, unzipping her white bubble jacket.

Passing the Salvation Army building, Sarah shouted at a man with white hair who was pushing a brush in the car park. He waved back before leaning on the brush. Moving on past the Jaguar showroom, they crossed the busy road and looked through the windows of the gym where students ran on treadmills.

Outside the pub they saw Kevin and John sitting at a table with a bottle of wine between them and, further up the road, beneath the cash point, Daz, leaning against the remains of a burned out plastic bin. 'Every fuckin' day he's there,' said Sarah.

They passed the off-licence, and waved through the open door to the owner, who smiled back at them from behind the till. At the bus stop, near the Aquatics Centre, students stood in a line, staring down the road. 'Can you spare any change, love?' said Sarah, to a girl with blonde pigtails.

'Erm . . . basically all I've got is my bus fare.'

'What about you, love?' said Sarah, to the man behind her.

'Sorry, mate.'

'Fuckin' . . . what about you?' she said to a Chinese student already shaking his head. 'God, you're a lot of tight bastards. Come on, Paul. Tight bastards.'

Walking away from the bus stop, they carried on down the road. Outside Blackwell's they sat down on some steps and asked nearly everyone that went past if they could spare some change. Some people said no, some made excuses and some just ignored them, but quite a few people delved into their purses or wallets or pockets for change, and by late afternoon Paul and Sarah had two cardboard cups full of coins to take into Spar.

'Can you give us a tenner for this, love?' said Sarah, tipping most of the change on the counter.

'I'll have to check with the manager.'

'Fuckin' 'ell. He knows us, you don't have to ask him.'

'I'll be back in a minute,' said the young assistant.

'Are you alright, love?' said Sarah, to the woman behind her in the queue.

'Fine, thanks. Just waiting my turn.'

'He won't be long. I don't suppose you could spare any change?'

'No, I can't.'

'Posh cow.'

'What?'

'Nothing. Hi, love. Alright?' said Sarah, to the returning shop assistant. 'I told you it would be alright, didn't a?' she said, as the shop assistant counted the change into the till and passed two crumpled fivers to Sarah. 'Cheers, love,' said Sarah, leaving the shop.

'You took you're fuckin' time didn't ya?' said Paul.

'Oh, shut up.'

They walked back down the road, past the rush hour traffic stopped at lights. Passing bus after bus, they peered up at all the faces that stared back from behind the dirty windows.

At the cash point they got some more change from a fresh-faced student who was waiting in the queue. As they crossed the road to the off licence, a man in a pale blue shirt pulled a shutter down over the doorway of the bank.

'That's twelve pounds please,' said the owner of the off licence, stifling a yawn and smiling.

'How much?' said Sarah.

'Twelve pounds,' he repeated.

'Very funny. We know you just make the fuckin' prices up. Here's a tenner and I want plenty of fuckin' change,' said Sarah.

'Would you like a bag?' he said, smiling.

'No thanks, love,' said Sarah, passing a bottle to Paul before counting her change and opening the door.

The tables chained to the pub wall opposite were filled with people soaking up the evening sunshine. A barmaid moved from table to table, stacking plastic pint pots into a pile that curved over her shoulder. Cigarette butts littered the floor and underneath one of the tables a black mongrel snoozed in the shade, its lead tied to a table leg.

'Fuckin' busy in there tonight,' said Paul.

'It's the weather, brings 'em all fuckin' out,' said Sarah.

'Yeah, a know.'

'Fuckin' shithole anyway.'

Going back past the gym, the students on treadmills looked out at them through the windows. Along the road, a red sightseeing bus went past with people in sunglasses taking pictures with mobile phones.

'Can you give us some of that change?' said Paul, as they crossed the road and passed the Jaguar showroom.

'What for?' said Sarah.

'I'm just going to use the phone.'

'What for?'

'Fuckin' hell. I'm phoning me dad up. It's his birthday.'

'Fuck him off.'

'Just give me some change.'

'Alright, here's a fuckin' quid. You soft cunt,' said Sarah, passing him a pound coin.

As he walked towards the phone box, Paul looked back at the Jaguar showroom. The car park gate opened and staff drove away in their cars. In the phone box, Paul put the money in and dialled the number, but there was no answer. He tried again, but there was still no response, so he put the pound coin in his pocket. In the next box along he saw Tracy, talking into the phone and playing with her blond hair. When she saw him looking in at her she waved for him to wait, and when she'd finished talking she came outside.

'Alright, Paul, stinks of piss in there,' she said, pulling up her knee-length brown boots.

'Yeah. You must be warm in them.'

'A know, but they love it, don't they. Where's Sarah?'

'She's gone back up.'

'Why don't we go for a walk?' said Tracy.

'Where to?'

'Just come with me for a bit. I've not spoke to ya in ages.'

'Alright.'

'Hey! Paul! Paul!' shouted Sarah from high in the tower block.

'Fuckin' Jesus . . . I'm just going for a walk!' he shouted back.

'Keep your fuckin' hands off, you!' she shouted.

'Oh, fuck off!' shouted Tracy. 'Come on, let's go.'

'Yeah, alright. She's going to be watching us all the way down there.'

'Don't worry about it, we'll be round the corner in a bit.'

Tracy finished the bottle that Paul had passed to her and dropped it onto the pavement. 'Let's sit down here' she said, pointing to a wooden bench in a tiny park beside the main road into town. As she sat down, Paul looked at the high heels of her boots that nestled among slivers of glass.

'You can't afford forty quid, love.'

'Don't you do freebies anymore, then?'

'Cheeky twat,' she said. 'There'll be loads out tonight. Fuckin' loads of 'em.'

'Come on . . . '

'Alright, alright, come over here then,' she said, walking behind some bushes and bending forward to rest her hands against a tree.

'Do you want to get a drink?' said Paul, afterwards.

'Nah. I'll get a smoke in a bit,' she said, smoothing the creases in her skirt.

'Cheers for that.'

'You're a cheeky twat. You know that?' she said, as a car horn beeped from the main road. 'Fuckin' 'ell. It's Tom. Gotta go, love. I'll see you later, alright?' she said, running through the park and getting into the back of a big silver car.

As the car moved away, Paul watched two magpies swooping over a group of pigeons. Then the magpies flew up into the trees as the pigeons continued to peck at a slice of bread. Beneath the trees, a man in a luminous jacket lifted paper and cans from the grass. By the fence, another man put signs up for concert parking. A burglar alarm filled the air, briefly joined by a car alarm. Across the road a billboard rattled around and, as Paul waited to cross, a long white limousine went past with a pink balloon shivering outside a tinted window.

'Took your fuckin' time didn't ya!' shouted Sarah, as soon as he came within sight of the flats. 'Just a blow-job was it!'

'Yeah! That's right! Just fuck off!' he said, before going into the phone box. He put the pound coin in and dialled the number again, but there was still no answer, so he put the pound coin back in his pocket and crossed the road to the flats.

Their balcony door was open, so the front door slammed shut behind him in the breeze. Sarah was sitting outside, the gold light of the evening sun glowing through the brown bottle wedged between her knees.

'Fuckin' warm on 'ere,' said Sarah, passing the bottle to Paul as he sat down next to her.

'Yeah,' said Paul.

'You told him 'appy birthday, then?'

'Yeah,'

'Soft cunt,' said Sarah, as the sunset disappeared behind the Beetham Tower.

MAGALUF

Summer floats over us; heat drifting slowly like a heart shaped balloon. The garden is filled with the cheap perfume of beer, and cigarette smoke disappears into the waning day, harmless to passive trees. Pete's coming back with the round, and when I look at him I realize he's still a big bastard, in fact, much bigger than the summer evening sixteen years ago when I first saw him lumbering over the fields with a cricket bat, Colin dwarfed beside.

The three of us have met up for the first time in ages. We no longer live near each other like we did when we'd go out every Friday to a pub in Ashton called The Birch, the time when we'd just left school and had started drinking pints, naively excited at being under age.

Pete's divorced with two kids now, one of whom, Kelly, had infant arthritis that required many operations in the first months and years of her young life. Colin's one of the oldest swingers in town, with a trendy haircut that hides his receding hairline, unless it's windy like today; a man of great vanity who's biggest worry in life, now that his parents have both died, is concealing the subtle rise of his man breasts.

The afternoon has passed-by, filled with prams and pushchairs, and all that remains is the long evening stretching out, absent of crying and bother. I look around at the swings becoming still, their shadows like the shade beneath lifted logs, and then up at the trees, the leaves crisping minutely above the white fenced enclosure.

'Bar's still fuckin' hammered,' says Pete, 'that big fucker behind the bar is slow as fuck. Anyway,' he says, putting three lagers on the table.

'Ahh, quality,' says Colin, 'Paul Weller, hits the spot.'

'Tell you something, that barmaid's nice. She looks a bit like that Keira Knightley, you know, the actress. *Pride and Prejudice* and all that,' I say.

'Fuckin' pride and fuckin' prejudice. You tart. Do you sit down to piss these days or what?' says Colin.

'I'm just saying she's beautiful, that's all.'

'She's called Emma, anyway,' says Pete.

'God, it's no wonder you never get a shag,' says Colin.

'When was the last time you spent more than one night with a bird?' says Pete.

'Hey, I don't need your ball and chain, oh, right, yeah, forgot. How many years on the mortgage? Another twenty. Fuckin' hell, this is about the first time we've seen you since you tubbed her and got shacked up,' says Colin.

'How do you work that one out? Kelly was born two years after we got married,' says Pete.

'Not my fault you were firing blanks is it?' says Colin.

I drink from my pint, and it tastes like nectar. I've been out quite a lot over the last week and I can tell it's one of those days when I'll be able to drink and drink and drink—but never get drunk. If you drink enough that happens, and if you've nothing else in life to feel good about, it can give you the illusion that because everyone else has fallen by the wayside you're somehow superior.

Because it's virtually the same as it's always been, I let the piss-taking banter go over my head. It's only when you leave Manchester that you realize how perfectly the sarcasm fits the accent, but a lifetime of it makes limitation light up like a cheap neon sign. I know Pete will wind us up all night unless I say something. 'When are you going to tell us what you dragged us out here for?' I ask.

'Just wanted to meet up with my old mates for a beer, what's wrong with that?'

'Nothing. I'm not saying there's anything wrong with it. I'm just saying why did you phone us both after all these years?'

'Well, the thing is, the old man died last week, and before he popped his clogs he asked me what you were up to.'

'Fuckin' hell, shit. Sorry, mate. No wonder,' I say.

'Shit, man. Come here, mate,' says Colin, putting his arms around Pete.

'Get off,' says Pete.

'Sorry, mate, just wanted to show my condolences,' says Colin.

'Well, you can do that at the funeral. We need a couple of big lads to carry the old bastard's coffin. He was a right fat bastard when his ticker gave out the first time, but he still wouldn't give up the fry-ups. Stubborn old bastard,' says Pete.

'When is it, then?' I ask.

'Not this Monday, the Monday after. You both alright to come? Ducki Crem, same place as the old queen,' says Pete.

'I'll be there,' I say.

'Yeah, me too. We can have a few beers after all, can't we? I'll get the old whistle and flute on, the birds love that,' says Colin.

'You don't fuckin' try and pull at a funeral,' says Pete.

'Listen, life goes on, mate,' says Colin.

'You're fuckin' priceless,' I say. 'Haven't you sowed your wild oats yet?'

'Will never happen, mate, not while there's still juice in the plums. Anyway, talking about oats, time you got the oat sodas in, your round,' says Colin, tilting his empty pint towards me, the sun glinting around the hula-hoop rim.

I'm usually reluctant with rounds, and if possible I'll try and get anyone else to go, but I'm keen to see the barmaid. She's a real beauty and reminds me of a barmaid I once knew, a girl I might have married had not her workplace been the storehouse for my downfall.

As so often happens, I'm served by the big bloke with the goatee beard and can only glance down the bar at Emma. As she pulls a pint I notice how tiny her elbow is, a pale white bone, smaller than the palm of my hand. Beard-face dumps the change on the bar and I make my way back outside, spilling the territory with booze.

'Here, have you heard of him?' asks Pete, as I put the pints on the table.

'Who?'

'That new hip hop star from Bradford?'

'What?'

'Ice T Wainwright . . .'

'What?'

'Ice T Wainwright.'

'. . . That's the single worst fucking joke that I have ever heard.'

'Hey, he's been years coming up with that,' says Colin.

'Time well spent. You never could tell jokes. What was that one about Drambuie, the one where you told the punch line first?' I ask.

'Some kind of fancy licker,' Pete and Colin mumble, in unison.

It's dark now, the black tree's branches drooping like a drunk's arms above the trampled grass. Only the three of us remain outside and our table is full of pint pots, empty, save for the remnants of lager that hug to the insides like phlegm.

Emma was never coming out to a table of three drunken blokes closer to middle age than teen age, but after closing time I catch a last glimpse of her through the tall windows of the pub, sitting between two red table lamps, savouring a longed-for cigarette, her black hair loosened from its bob and falling on her light white shoulders. I know that if she were wearing them, there'd be at least one ladder in her tights.

Pete falls head-first over the glowing white picket fence, while Colin hurdles it before clutching a hamstring. I go out through the gate, the maestro of hindsight that I am, and we make our way back to Pete's empty house.

Colin barges past me and runs up the stairs to grab the spare room, while I look at the five feet long couch on which I'll incubate my hangover throughout the night. As my eyes adjust to the darkness, I can make out the black blobs on a white background of what I remember to be a picture of Pete's children. I knew it was a bad idea to come back. It's alright for Colin, who barely ever sleeps in his own bed anyway, but for me, a light sleeper at the best of times, it's the guarantee of a night filled with circuitous thinking.

The last time the three of us spent any significant amount of time together was sixteen years ago, when we went on holiday to Magaluf in Majorca, Spain. We were all eighteen, on our first holidays without our parents, and all virgins, despite what we told each other at the time.

On the first afternoon we went down to the pool with the intention of having a couple of pints and saving ourselves for later, but we ended up getting drunk by about five and falling asleep in the sun chairs.

Later on, outside the Red Lion, a Geordie DJ called the Brown Hatter interrupted old records with even older jokes. On our way in he shouted, 'Hello, virgins!' but our sunburned faces couldn't have blushed anymore, the red rushing to our cheeks like blood inside red balloons.

The music blared out across the beer garden and over the thin stretch of car-less road to another English pub opposite, and fitted our mood of optimism for the week ahead.

> *Hey Mr Postman look and see, oh yeah . . .*
> 'Hello, whities!' interrupted the DJ.
> *What it is that you're coming to see?*
> 'What would you be doing at home now? Sunday night?'
> *Mr Po-o-o-ostman, look and see, oh yeah . . .*
> 'Watching the Antiques fuckin' Roadshow.'
> *Wait a minute, wait a minute, ooh yeah . . .*
> 'I'd love to go on that'
> *Mr Po-o-o-ostman, oh yeah,*
> 'Tell 'em it's worth fuck all! More whities, hello!'

After a few more pints we went to Magaluf's biggest nightclub, BCM's. We got free t-shirts on the way in and then wandered around the vast hangar, laser lights criss-crossing us in petrol rainbow colours, teenagers blowing whistles and dancing all around like frantic monkeys with dandruff and bright white teeth.

I'd never seen Pete dance before, but he really went for it, hundreds of miles away from home and inhibition, the three or four pints of Tennant's Extra and the Birch jukebox. Arms flailing, he twisted in a violent circle, and people began to copy him until he ploughed through a table.

I pulled that night. Why else do you think I'm telling you all this? She'd been one of those people copying Pete, and when Pete sat down she started dancing with Colin. When she asked me why I wasn't dancing, I said I couldn't be arsed. She was a cockney, and I soon realized that I no longer disliked the accent.

When we left BCM's, Jen came with us, along with her friend, Vicky, who'd spent the preceding two hours drinking pints of lager with Pete but seemed to have taken it better. After Pete and Colin wandered off on a game that involved ripping the wing mirrors off cars, I walked Vicky and Jen back to their hotel in nearby Palma Nova.

Once inside, Vicky disappeared almost immediately and Jen jumped on me, sticking her tongue down my throat. She seemed even more determined to get something out of the way than I did, and when she turned me on my back and then accidentally sat down on me, the pain was so overbearing that the word detumescence barely does it justice.

When I made my way back to the hotel in the morning, my melancholy left me susceptible to the visions of farce that lay waiting. I found Pete masturbating in front of the mirror with an expression on his face that suggested a case of lock–jaw, an expression that relaxed as markedly as everything else when he saw my face smirking in the reflection. Colin sat on the toilet, the door wide open and the smell wafting into a room already fouled by spilt beer, fag ash, burger meat and the post-massacre of spilt chilli. Underpants hung from the TV, and a sound of dripping came from the corner, where someone had vomited directly onto a lamp. The balcony doors were open and there was a puddle beneath the rail, the hot summer sun glinting gold on yellow, and the strains of the *A Team* music blasting into our heads and calling for a sarcastic riposte that none of us could be bothered to utter.

From the couch in the corner I saw the dishevelled figure of a very young woman, blowing cigarette smoke rings in a dissipating tunnel above her head, naked from the waist down and knees in the air like she was about to give birth to a lager fart, which duly came. When I asked her who she was, she requested that I 'shut the fuck up' and stick my 'two-quid sunglasses' up my 'lubed arse'.

Magaluf

On the table there was a plastic tub of cola, absent of fizz and diluted by long-melted ice, and I drank it all down before going to the bedroom, where I fell on the bed and rolled off down the narrow gap between the bed and the wall, remaining there until some time later when I woke to the strains of *Welcome to the Jungle*, my head feeling ready to crack in half and my back aching as if it had been run over by a zealous lunatic on a rickshaw.

Colin was going on about having a full English breakfast, and when Pete joined in I succumbed. Nobody mentioned the girl on the couch with the mouth of a sailor and a gorgeous self-possession. Sitting in the too-hot morning sun, eating fried bread and pouring tea across a tongue that felt covered in flour, I thought about Jen, her smooth white body the greatest thing I'd ever touched, and wondered where she'd lose her virginity. I thought then that she'd be one of many such intimacies, but now I look back and wonder at the profligacy of a boy who knew nothing.

In the afternoon we caught the bus out to the water park. Colin was like a child dragging us up the steps to the top of the slides where we stood queuing and shivering in the wind. An officious attendant made us wait in turn and I watched Colin and Pete disappear down the plastic chute before going myself, sliding through the pipe and flailing out into the pool like a turd slapping into the sea, where a waiting Colin and Pete grabbed me and repeatedly ducked my head under the water.

We went on ride after ride, the thrill of the slides and the fleeting perversion of the stairs ridding us all of our hangovers. Exhausted, we lay our towels on a strip of hot concrete and slumped in the shade of off-white parasols, our burnt bodies cooling like car engines in the early evening breeze.

On the way back to the hotel I got a crate of Beck's that I put in the fridge, then had a shower that burst out in coughs of hard water. When I came out I saw Colin standing on the balcony in a thong, his arse cheeks weighted to one side like a drunk slowly falling.

'What the fuck is that you've got on,' I said.

'The birds will love it, mate. Come here,' he said, motioning me towards the balcony.

'Look at that.'

With just the towel around my waist I looked down, and directly beneath the balcony a young woman lay topless on her back, body caramel and nipples nougat pink. Colin whipped off my towel and threw it over the balcony, where it landed soundlessly and waited for the passing flip-flops of the morning's first German.

That night, and for the rest of the week, we found it progressively more difficult to get drunk, and the realization that we were no more able to chat women up in Magaluf than we were in England dawned on me and Pete long before Colin, who tried time and again, seemingly insensitive to rejection.

On the night before we left I was too knackered for another big night, and was content to nurse slow San Miguel's from a cool seat in the corner of the Red Lion's concrete beer garden, smiling at the same jokes the DJ told on our first night. Colin and Pete went to BCM's for one last time, and I waved to them as they walked past me down the street.

With my chair turned side-on to the DJ, I was able to watch all the people passing by. I saw a group of lads my age, dressed in almost identical white shirts left un-tucked, hair shiny with gel and faces flushed by the sun. It was a time when the binge drinking culture was being road tested by Brits abroad, and it was a while before it dawned on proprietors, then punters, that they didn't have to go to another country and put money into someone else's economy to create the illusion of escape.

I caught the DJ giving me a glance, and that brief moment of complicity was enough for him not to draw attention to my sitting alone. I picked a guidebook off the floor and read that within a few miles of where I was sitting, great swathes of countryside stretched out to the foot of a mountain range that gave panoramic views of a glittering sea.

When thoughts of home came, I felt largely relieved that I wouldn't have to go out again for a while, but I also felt the familiar melancholy at the end of any holiday, the forgotten knowledge about the brevity of the freedom that they bring.

Looking back out at the dark street I saw Jen and Vicky walking hand in hand with respective tall males, and when I caught Jen's eye she didn't seem to recognize me, instead turning to look up at her new man. I wondered if he was the reason she seemed more comfortable with herself, or whether it had been something they'd previously shared that made her walk with such carefree ease, seemingly sober and in no apparent rush to be anywhere other than where she was at that exact moment.

All the next day we sat with our suitcases by the pool, having had to be out of our rooms by ten that morning. Someone had pissed in the pool and the water had gone brown, and as we sat fully clothed on the sun chairs, the old Spanish barman from the poolside bar looked down into the draining depths and then back up at us, weariness in his sparkling, hooded eyes.

Pete stands waiting outside the church as I step out of the taxi, his bulk heightened by the broad shoulders of his suit. As I walk up to him I see that he's smiling, and when I shake his hand he says into my ear, 'Let's get this over with and get to the pub.'

As the coffin disappears, pushing through red velvet curtains like a child impatient for a film, I look next to me at a smiling Colin and struggle to contain myself beneath the recorded sounds of Pete's dad giving a strained rendition of *You Were Always On My Mind*. A woman at the back bursts out in a melodramatic wail, and it transpires that she's the Elvis fan he'd been on top of when his heart gave out in the sack.

Seeing our smiles, a small bloke dressed in white with a large medallion around his neck gives us the most remonstrative look possible from a face the double of comedy actor Rowan Atkinson, and I look down at the floor like a football fan barely able to avoid shouting during a minute's silence.

When the service is over I stand outside with Colin and am relieved at not having laughed. There was just something about the formality of the situation that made me feel giddy. As soon as Colin finishes his cigarette we look up at the smoke coming out of the chimney of the church, and give Pete's dad a rueful smile as he disappears into what's left of the ozone layer.

At the pub, we sit in a warm corner and wait to be joined by others dressed in black. The face of the barman with the goatee sinks when he realizes what he's seeing. Emma isn't here, which is a shame, because I've actually gotten to know her a little bit through tiny conversations that last as long as it takes to pull a pint.

Around me in the corner, the half dozen or so that chose to come from the church sip carefully from their drinks, the mood of mourning not yet affected one way or the other by booze. The woman who'd wailed during the service sits next to Colin, who keeps looking down at her stocking-covered thigh as she lifts her veil to sip cider. The only other people who've turned up are an old couple that keep slapping each other in the face. I don't know who they are, and my only guess is that they came to the wrong funeral.

At about eight, Emma turns up for her shift and I can't help smiling at her recognition of the motley gang before her. When I talk to her at the bar she seems more open than she's been before. Maybe it's my suit, or the fact that I've come from a funeral, but after last orders, she smokes her first cigarette while sitting next to me, the light from the red lamps striking the shiny black hair shaken from its bob.

She tells me she's been reading Plath and trying to write poems of her own. We talk and talk until her beauty seems to come more from within than without, and when I ask her for her phone number, she says she'll think about it, retaining the secrecy of her heart at the same time as a faint smile tries to give it away. As she gets up to go to the toilet I notice Colin in the corner, his head moving slowly beneath a veil. Alongside, Pete is just sitting there and staring at the wall, the pub silent save for the sound of kissing lips.

THE LAST POST

Steve put on his white overalls, knee-high yellow plastic boots, hair net and white dairyman's hat, before finally putting on a blue beard-snood and going on to the shop floor, where he washed his hands in a silver sink that looked like a long urinal, and made his way to the line for two minutes before six.

Beneath the bright white light he watched as other staff shuffled in, past the line managers wearing white fedoras with red bands and holding clipboards as props. As soon as everyone arrived at the line, the work began. Steve waited with an open box by the moving conveyor as, at the head of the line, rashers of bacon were piled in fives and moved down a strip of rolling black plastic, where they disappeared beneath the silver hulk of the packing machine and re-emerged on the other side, shrink wrapped and labelled. Two people standing on either side then put them into boxes before passing them to Steve, who slid them under the tape machine and put them on the conveyor. The conveyor then took them around the perimeter of the shop floor and up above the corridor between the shop floor and the loading bay, until finally they reached the loading bay itself, where they were stacked on pallets and loaded onto wagons.

During the eight-hour shift, shop floor staff had a half hour lunch break, plus two breaks of seven and a half minutes, one before lunch and one after. In the canteen most of the staff chose to eat the same kind of bacon that surrounded them all day.

~

At the airport in Kingston, Steve got off the plane first and was followed by Derek and Ann, Roger and Emily, Eddie and Sandra, and finally Lee and Sue. They descended the steps off the plane and were met by the tour guide who showed them onto a coach full of other cricket fans come to support England for what was expected to be a tightly fought series.

On the day of the match they got to Sabina Park early and sat side-on to the pitch, near a peanut seller throwing bags into the crowd. They set up their deck chairs and cool boxes, slapped on sun cream, fiddled with hats and sunglasses, tuned in the radio and sat back to soak up the sun as it was announced that the West Indies had won the toss and put England in to bat. A few minutes later the umpires emerged in their white coats, followed by the West Indies team and then, accompanied by the roars of the Barmy Army, the England openers ran onto the outfield, practising shots and nervously adjusting pads and gloves.

England lost three quick wickets on a pitch of pace and erratic bounce. Batsmen were hit on the gloves, box, arms and helmet, and on more than one occasion the umpires came together for a conference. In the stand behind them, a Jamaican with a frizzy grey beard played the last post on a conch shell, and behind him another local man, wearing a red dress, hung from the rafters like a gymnast, unashamedly flashing frilly knickers. The crowd were in hysterics as the man in the dress jumped down and picked up his own bat to display a loose-limbed forward defensive that mocked the England batsmen, and no one saw it coming when it was announced that the match was to be abandoned.

'I don't believe this. I've been wanting to do this for years, and the first time I come here they cancel the match after a few overs. Never happened before. Can you believe that?' said Derek.

'Well, there was something wrong with the pitch. We'd have been all out for fifty anyway. The match would have been over in two days,' said Steve.

'Not if they'd prepared a proper pitch. It's just typical, me and Ann have been scrimping and saving for this, and I know Lee and Sue have, and everyone else. Now what are we going to do, sit around on the beach all week? I didn't save up for this. We're going to be buggered when we get back. I should be thinking of retirement soon. Jesus, just get me another rum will you, son, she's gone up to bed.'

'They all have,' said Steve.

'I only came for the cricket, son. The cricket.'

When Steve returned with the drink, Derek had reclined further into the long wicker chair, his bright Hawaiian shirt riding up and his beer belly sticking out like the curve of a large cheese. Steve put the glass on the table beside him, and they sat there with a view across the bay, the only sound coming from the same waves that led a diamond route to the tree covered hills.

'You know something,' said Derek, 'this should be the best week of my entire life. All winter I've been looking forward to this. It's alright for you, you're young, you've got your whole life to go places. For me, this was it.'

'Yeah, well, make the most of it. Age has nothing to do with it. What are you, fifty? You've got ages to retirement.'

'Fifty-two. Don't remind me, son. Listen, age *has* got something to do with it. You've your whole life ahead.'

'At a bacon factory.'

'Do something else then, while you can. Don't get tied down, at least while you can help it. The youth of today, I'm telling you. Useless. Don't wait until you get to my age.'

'You're not that old, though.'

'I am, son, believe me. I remember when I was a kid, I thought I was going to play for Lancashire, and then even when that didn't work out I always had this feeling in the back of my mind that I was different, that I wouldn't just have an ordinary life, that something would turn up.'

'You've got your family.'

'I know that, son. Look, I work every day of my life for them, clothe them, feed them, keep a roof over their heads, but it's not that I'm talking about. I'm fifty-two years old, and what have I done? Get some ambition, son, for god's sake.'

'Ambition? Coming here was your ambition.'

'This was supposed to be a great holiday. Maybe . . . well, it's like this holiday, as it turns out . . . best thing about it was the looking forward to it.'

'Yeah, well. I'm just going to get my own place. I know I'm young but . . . you've got to be realistic. Anything else that goes my way is just a bonus.'

'Don't say that, son,' said Derek, finishing his drink, 'don't say that.'

On the moonlit beach some local kids had started to play cricket and, as Derek shuffled off to bed, Steve got himself another rum and coke and watched as one of the kids played a hook shot high into the air, the yellow ball disappearing and then reappearing to land on a slowly flattening curve of black and silver.

On the second Monday back, Roger was off sick, so they were a man down on the line and Derek had to do the work of two men, filling the boxes on his own as they emerged from the silver hulk of the packing machine. Steve had to keep loading the boxes onto the ever-moving conveyor, and soon the packets of bacon began to pile up on the floor around Derek's feet, prompting one of the fedora-wearing line managers to march towards him.

'We can't have the bacon falling on the floor, it's against health and safety,' he said, as Derek continued to struggle.

'Yeah, well, Roger's off, I don't know if you've noticed.'

'I'm well aware of that, but we can't have the whole system grinding to a halt because you can't keep up.'

'Look, it's a two man job this, it needs two people here,' said Derek, as the packets continued to fall.

'Right, we'll sort this out,' said the line manager, prodding the red nose of the stop button. 'Steve, you come here and swap places for a moment.'

The line manager started the conveyor again and Steve worked hard to keep up, filling the boxes with the packets of bacon. Within minutes he felt sweat beginning to form on his back, but he was able to manage, and after a few minutes the line manager stopped the conveyor.

'If he can keep up, why can't you? If you are getting too old then we might have to think about moving you somewhere else. Have you folding the boxes or something. Now, unless you want that then you'd better keep up,' he said, pressing the red button as Derek resumed his position.

Eventually Derek was able to keep pace, even though his back was filled with pain. Steve kept his head down and put box after taped-up box on the conveyor, and when Derek looked at the clock he was glad to see that it was nearly break time.

CONFINED SPACES

They camped in a tent in Don's back garden, they played basketball in his garage, and after a while they began to hide in cupboards, once emerging from beneath the sink and frightening Don's mum so much that she dropped a piece of cake.

Having exhausted all the possibilities at Don's, which also included hiding in the loft, the cellar and the pantry, they started to explore Nick's house, first spending time in his dad's shed, where they found his stash of magazines, and then moving inside. First they tried the airing cupboard and found it too hot, then the loft, which was unconverted and cold and just waiting for a foot through the floor. Then Nick remembered the fireplace. The chimney had been blocked off, but there was still an oblong space behind the wooden fireplace that held the electric fire. Early one morning when his parents where still in bed, Nick slid the fireplace forward and inspected the musty confinement, glad to see that there was room for two.

Though Nick (and Don) would be going to secondary school the following year, Nick's parents still got a babysitter for him when they went to the Pack Horse on a Friday night, and when he got back from Don's, Suzanne would always be sitting there on the couch, either with a boyfriend or another girl come to keep her company and root through the fridge for food and booze.

One Friday night, Nick and Don hid in Nick's garden and

waited for the bathroom light to go on before rushing in the back door, sliding out the fireplace and sneaking in behind it.

When Suzanne came back down, she sat on the couch and flicked through the TV channels, letting out a bored sigh before turning it off. Then they heard the tiny presses of her text messaging before she got up and began to look at herself in the mirror directly above the fireplace. From their concealment they could see the underside of her chin, and frowned when they realized she was squeezing a spot.

After playing with her hair for what seemed an interminable time, she began to eat from a box of chocolates on the table. They heard her chewing and giggled to each other before squinting nervously through the gap to see if she'd heard them. She hadn't, and when she sat back and turned on the TV they felt their legs begin to ache in the tiny space.

After a while someone knocked on the front door and Nick and Don slid the fireplace forward a little before panicking and scrambling back. The sound of two voices, one markedly deeper than the other, began coming closer down the hallway. They heard kissing, and soon realized that Suzanne was with Simon Brown from Norlan Avenue. The kissing seemed to continue for hours, until Suzanne went to the kitchen and dragged a bottle from the bottom of the fridge. Nick and Don heard the glugging of the wine going into the glasses and then nothing else, until Suzanne shouted at Simon.

'Oh, come on,' said Simon.

'Come on, what?' said Suzanne.

'We've got the whole house to ourselves here. Come on, why don't we go upstairs and go on a bed?'

'No! And anyway, Nick should have been back by now, I'm going to phone Don's parents, make sure he's still there.'

'Oh, fuck him. Little shit.'

'Don't! Don't talk about him like that. God, I don't believe you. Is that the only reason you came here, just to get me upstairs?'

'No, Suze, don't be silly. I just can't help it, you know, all the kissing and everything. I'm only human.'

'Okay, okay. Well, just be quiet while I give them a call.'

'Alright, sorry, Suze.'

From behind the fireplace they heard Suzanne dial the number and say, 'Hi, Mrs Rickett? Yeah, hi it's Suzanne, is err . . . is Nick still over there? . . .'

'No? . . .'

'Well, do you have any idea . . .'

'No, no, okay, well I'll let you know when they come in . . .'

'Yes, okay, thanks. Right, okay, yes, bye Mrs Rickett . . .'

'I wonder where those little turds have got to,' said Simon.

'Don't!' said Suzanne.

'Oh, you know I'm only joking. Come here,' said Simon.

Soon they began kissing again. Don and Nick felt one or more parts of their body going numb and, when Nick needed to cough, he had to clamp his mouth shut with his hands.

'Okay, calm down, calm down, they're going to be back in a minute,' said Suzanne.

'Listen, is the back door locked? I'm going to bolt it, then the little turd will have to knock if he wants to get in,' said Simon.

'Yeah, but then we'll have to get up.'

'Well I'll get it, don't you worry.'

When Simon came back from the kitchen he stood above her by the couch. She smiled up at him but he pushed her shoulders so that she fell back, and as the smile on her face disappeared, he undid his jeans and started pulling at hers. When she wouldn't yield he pulled harder and harder, pressing against her and ignoring her shouts, and soon he'd got the jeans down to her knees and was tugging at her knickers, and was almost inside her when the fireplace suddenly moved and Nick and Don crawled out, flexing their knees.

'What the fuck is going on?' said Simon.

'Fuck off, Simon,' said Nick.

'Yeah, fuck off,' said Don, as Simon pulled up his pants and rushed over to grab Nick by the throat.

'Get off him! Get off!' said Suzanne.

'Fucking little shits! If either of you say a fucking word about this I'll kick your fucking heads in. Right?' said Simon, before rushing off.

'I don't know what the hell you were doing behind there. You better go home Don, your mum will be worried sick,' said Suzanne.

'Okay, sorry, Suzanne,' said Don.

'It was just a game,' said Nick, feeling like he was going to cry.

'Hey, come here,' she said, before giving him a hug.

When Nick's parents came back in he heard one of his mum's high heels fall off as she stumbled up the stairs. He turned away and squeezed his eyes shut as the door opened and the light from the landing passed over him on the bed. He smelt the red wine on her breath as she kissed him on the cheek. Later, still awake, he held both hands to his ears.

When Nick and Don met the following day, they played kerby on the avenue. They each stood on either side of the road, taking it in turns to throw the ball at the kerb so that it might bounce back to them. When Nick got one to come back he walked forward for his three easier goes from the middle of the road, but then had to jump back onto the pavement when Simon accelerated towards him in a car.

'What a cheese-dick,' said Don.

'Yeah. What a bell-end!' said Nick, as they both laughed and made V signs for Simon to see in his rear view mirror.

Nick was 9–3 in front by the time Simon came speeding back up the road with Suzanne in the passenger seat, and it was only a few months later that they both watched from the tree in Nick's garden as Suzanne, dressed all in white, climbed into the back of a much bigger car.

RETAIL THERAPY

Danny sat down on a bench, looked dazedly at the early morning sky, the clouds blue ink in Guinness, and sank back onto the bench to sleep. Before he slipped away he felt himself grabbed by the coat collar, lifted to his feet and punched in the stomach. He fell over, bounced off the side of the bin and landed on the muddy grass, and when he raised his head off the floor a boot kicked it straight back down, cracking his nose and sending blood idling down his face and dripping more quickly from the chin. He felt hands in his pockets and his ring finger wrenched. He was kicked repeatedly in the stomach, causing him to vomit puke and blood. Eyes blurred and shaky from pain, he could just see his attackers running away, their hoods and jeans disappearing out of the park.

He woke with a terrier standing on his cheek and sniffing his hair, and then listened to it pissing against the bench inches from his head. Blinking in the bright early sunlight he saw the passing feet of the dog's owner and heard the utterance of 'fucking winos'.

The pub was shot through with the light of the morning, the sun insistent through windows and cigarette smoke rising like a fishing net across a shoal of red faced punters. Danny saw shop staff, their garish uniforms not quite hidden beneath jackets, a couple of road workers, and a wino sitting by the radiator with an empty half on the table and a carrier bag between his feet. When Danny finished his whisky he went to the bathroom, lifted up his shirt and saw a series of bruises that dotted his chest like the hoof prints of a cow.

When he came back out Danny asked the barman for the phone book, then looked up the number for his bank and gave them a call from the payphone at the end of the bar.

'Another large one, Jason—when you're ready. No, no, in your own time, son,' said Danny, after the call.

'There you go, Danny.'

'Cheers.'

'Not working then today?'

'No, not my turn this week.'

'Right.'

'Thanks for the phone book.'

'No problem.'

'I had to phone the bank.'

'Right.'

'Got robbed last night.'

'Yeah?'

'My own fault, I suppose. My own fault.'

'Have you phoned the police?'

'The police? Waste of time, son. They've got better things to worry about than some loser whose wife has left him. You know, I saw her the other day with that cunt.'

'Yeah, well,' said Jason, leaning at the end of the bar.

'Have you got a girlfriend, Jason?'

'Yeah.'

'Well, don't trust her. You might think she's loves you now, son.'

'They aren't all like . . .'

'. . . Like what? My wife? Or should I say, ex-wife?'

'I don't know, Danny, I never met her, did I?'

'Lucky for you, son.'

'Yeah, well,' said Jason, moving off to serve.

In the afternoon Danny went to the bank and took some money out over the counter. Then he went to the off licence and bought himself a can of coke, a loaf of white bread and a bottle of Bell's.

At home he made himself some toast and a whisky and coke, then sat down in front of the TV. He laughed at a programme where people who were no good at sport tried to play sport—the premise being because they were not-quite-forgotten celebrities it would be entertaining.

He turned off the TV and managed to resist kicking it over, and then went over to his vinyl collection to pick out some music. All the album covers seemed to have her fingerprints on them, and when he picked up *Goat's Head Soup*, he looked at Mick Jagger on the cover, face wrapped in a yellow muslin haze, and scraped the needle across the grooves to *Angie*.

In the morning he cleared away all the empty beer cans and whisky bottles and sat for a moment in the chair. He got up again and washed all the dishes in the sink, watching out of the window as two crows crossed the winter sky, their languid black wings falling and rising like the arms of a conductor in quiet moments of Mahler.

Danny had been a regular at the old fashioned barber's. He sat on the one remaining empty chair, nearest the door, and watched as the slow recognition of the old man's glances changed from slighted to smiling. He picked up the local newspaper and read about the team he'd once played football for as a promising junior, and then looked out through the window at the people and the traffic passing between the barber's and the same old butcher's shop opposite.

In the chair, covered by a blue shroud and a towel tucked roughly into his collar, Danny smiled up at the younger barber, told him what he wanted, and barely noticed any response before his head was shoved gently sideways. With his chin resting on clippings of lopped fringe, he felt the languid approach of sleep as the razor tickled and tapered his neck hair.

The man in the seat next to him made sarcastic jokes about 'the wife', saying that she had a 'bloody stopwatch running' every time he left the house. The old barber, deaf as the wind-twirled stripes outside, asked him to repeat what he'd just said, but he didn't, and instead just told the barber to 'turn the bloody thing up.'

'We've not seen you for a while?' said the younger barber, to Danny.

'No, no, I thought you'd not remembered me.'

'I remember everyone's head, you know.'

'Right.'

'How's the wife?'

'She's alright, I suppose. Haven't seen her for a while.'

'Why's that then?'

'She left me.'

'Bloody hell, I'm sorry, mate.'

'You weren't to know, don't worry. Anyway, it was a while ago now.'

'Well . . .'

' . . . Yeah.'

'Maybe she's done you a favour. Go out and enjoy your freedom,' said the younger barber, trimming Danny's sideboards.

'Yeah . . . a favour, yeah, you might be right there.'

'Dead right, you can do all the things she wouldn't let you do now.'

'Yeah, maybe, but there wasn't anything really. I was happy.'

'These things happen for a reason, you know.'

'Yeah. Did you ever get married?'

'Me? No.'

'Why not?'

'I've got my mother to look after.'

'Right.'

'Eighty-two and still dancing, just like him over there. He'll be in the pub 'till all hours later.'

'How old is he?'

'The same—neither of them will ever pop their clogs.'

'Heh, heh.'

'What's that he's saying?' asked the old barber.

'Nothing, Lawrence, nothing.'

After going to the place behind The Last Orders, Danny caught the bus to the giant shopping mall on the outskirts of town, where he sat drinking coffee in a plastic seat beside a waterfall. Around him, ornate pink pillars rose to the glass ceiling, supporting the giant structure of a rose-coloured mall that stretched for miles, the walls and floors and elevators and stairs —the whole grand monotony—differentiated only by the colours of the signs on shop units.

He went into a bookshop where all the staff wore black and repeatedly hassled any unwitting browsers, and counted a block of two hundred autobiographies by a twenty-year-old footballer.

He wanted a can of coke, and searched the mall's miles before reaching a Boot's that only had the more expensive bottles. Every five minutes a sinister voice reminded people that it was forbidden to smoke in the building, and camera after camera twitched in the artificial light.

Danny watched a giant TV screen with bullet points moving right to left in a blue ribbon beneath a picture of another busy shopping centre. He kept looking back, face bathed in the digital glow.

Finishing his coke, he made another trip around the mall, until his eyes began to ache. Suddenly he got short of breath, and had to sit down to compose himself. Opposite, a giant frog blasted out a ring tone for a mobile phone, and Danny felt for the gun. Then, with a start, he got up and searched for the exit.

Outside, Danny stared out across the shiny roofs of a thousand and more cars. He saw buses crammed with bags, heads peeping out of the windows from just above, and tried to follow their route. At the exit a vast monolith of a giant man in a suit stood in the posture of applause, and an even bigger sign beside him told customers to come back.

Danny walked along a grass verge past a cereal factory and through the industrial estate. Leaving the estate behind, he entered the suburbs and, as soon as he could, moved away from the bus-routed roads.

He sat on a swing in a park, his feet like the wind-blown shadows of sunflowers across the tarmac. Seeing a group of children on the other side of the field, he walked out of the park and onto the canal bank, where he bent down and placed the gun gently through the surface of the water.

He gazed around at the disused factory units either side of the canal, hundreds of black oblongs where their windows had been. Above them stood an empty gasholder, bright as a rattle in grass. Further along, a duck submerged its head in the canal before re-emerging to float alone beneath the overhanging branches of a pink freckled tree.

ALL SMILES SAVED

I've got to go and sign on and it's the only day of the fortnight where I have to be somewhere I don't want to be. Getting out of the lift, I leave the building and walk to Oxford Road, past all the students waiting for buses back to Rusholme and Fallowfield and Withington. I pass Manchester Metropolitan, then Manchester University, and sit for a time in Whitworth Park, where I can smell the cheap beer clutched in a wino's hand.

After walking past some hoodies by the door of the Job Centre, I'm hit by a wave of dry sweat and the sound of a young woman berating a member of staff. A security guard gets up from her table and wanders across the carpet to put a hand on the woman's shoulder. All around the room people are trying to ignore each other, including staff with emotionless faces, faces changed by abuse from open to defensive, all smiles saved for the moment they leave the building.

When my name is called I go over and sit down at the desk. The assistant registers my presence from the corner of his eye before focusing back on the computer.

'How's your job search going?' he says, eyes still on the screen.

'I keep looking,' I answer.

'Are you still looking for teaching jobs and retail?'

'Yeah.'

'Well, as you've been signing on for six months we need to start expanding the range of jobs you apply for. I'll just check what's on the system,' he says, before I can reply.

'Okay, well, there's nothing for bookshops, but there are a few retail jobs. There's one here to work in a video shop in Moss Side. Five pounds an hour, must be available evenings and weekends. I'll just print out the details for you. I won't be a minute,' he says, getting up from the desk and walking over to the printer.

As he comes back I notice he's called KENNY. He passes me the printout and also my book, which I sign. After he's done what he has to, he gives the book back, and when I say 'Thanks, Kenny' he looks at me like I've slapped him out of a sleepwalk, and it's the first eye contact we've made.

When I get up to leave I look at the waiting line. There's a black guy hunched over with his elbows on his knees, heels bouncing up and down on the floor, a skinny bloke with tattooed arms, rolling a cigarette, a woman with earrings like giant bubbles, a man in his fifties with a greasy quiff and a boozer's red nose, a man with gel in his hair alternately reading job pages and looking up at the clock (a new claimant), two girls who look like they've just left school, both talking on mobiles, and a young man in a baseball cap, fondling a gold bracelet on his wrist.

As the doors shut behind me I feel my shoulders loosen—I've never been much of an actor, so looking keen was difficult. Screwing the printout into a ball, I volley it into the air six times, a new record.

For years I worked at a factory in Ashton-Under-Lyne, standing at a conveyor belt and loading pallets up with boxes of sausages. Five of us stood in line, watching the boxes as they sidled along the conveyor, turned a corner and slid down the slope, the cardboard brushing over the metal runners, loud as traffic. It was a refrigerated area, so I'd be wearing a heavy coat and trousers, gloves and a woolly hat, even in mid-summer. Every time I lifted a box off the conveyor and put it on the pallet I had to turn around straight away to catch the next one, or else the boxes would jam up.

Directly behind the pallet there was a heated office where the supervisors sat, reading from newspapers or laughing and joking with each other. If I caught their eye they'd stick two fingers up, or point at the moving conveyor. Behind them was a giant clock that I couldn't help noticing every time I stacked a box.

When a pallet was full I had to shrink wrap it, so I'd pick up a wrap the size and shape of a rolling pin, tuck some of it under the corner of a box and run round and round, wrapping it as tight as possible so the fork lifts could pick up the pallet.

The shift was 3–11, and some nights when I worked overtime I'd stand alone by the cold conveyor until two in the morning, the boxes barely a trickle and the clock getting slower and slower.

I go to the nearest cash point on Wilmslow Road and walk away from the curry mile. Weaving through the crowds outside the Student Union, I notice how I'm one of the few people not offered a flyer. Near the bookshop there's a university building with a connecting walkway stretching high over Oxford Road. Going under it reminds me of being on a bus with my dad on the way to and from City—little did I know then that I'd be living around here and signing on the rock n' roll.

Pondering that, I go to the Salutation for a drink. It's just off Oxford Road, hidden from the buses by a university building, and as ever it's filled with a mixture of students and locals. There's always an edge to the atmosphere, as though armed raiders came yesterday, but I like that; I'd rather see a fight than a fashion show. There's something about being here on a Monday afternoon that makes me feel like an outlaw, free from the working posse.

I look at my golden pint, and then pick it up and start drinking. I could easily down it in one, because I love the taste so much, but I make the effort not to. On the sports pages of a newspaper left on the table next to me, the headline reads: GOATER SINKS REDS, and I think about Maine Road.

Pushing through the rusty turnstile and into the ground behind dad, I wait while he buys a shiny blue programme. We climb up the grey steps into the Kippax. Halfway up the stand we go down a white tunnel, and the ground gradually appears, first the blue seats in the Main Stand opposite, then the advertising boards, and then the magic expanse of green, with the players warming up—the coach sending crosses over for the keeper to catch in his yellow-trimmed gloves, and the rest doing shuttle runs from the touchline to the centre, the heels of their black boots kicking up soil. I sit on a blue metal stanchion, above the same faces that surround us every game: the man who passes a silver hip flask around, the man who stands on a wooden box with ORANGES on it, the man in black who stutters, the man in brown who takes the piss out of the man who stutters, the man with a black moustache who shouts abuse at the referee for the whole game, the man with the blue flask who takes sarcasm to new heights and can barely clap his red hands.

Looking back at my golden pint, I think of how scared I was of dad when I was a child. The more like him I became the less we got on, but eventually we mellowed out and learned to trust each other again. I always pictured him as he was in an old photograph I had. A black and white shot, it showed him playing football in his twenties. He had a beard and long hair, and was bursting between two players with the ball at his feet, rampaging towards the opposition goal. He looked totally and utterly fearless, and that gave a real poignancy to his final days, when the only life came from his eyes, blue as a brand new City shirt.

I haven't had a permanent full time job for ten years. When I did work, I used to think people on the dole were all skiving bastards that I was paying taxes for, although in the back of my mind I'm sure I must have known that economics is more complex than that.

Finishing my beer, I go home to pick up my guitar. I play it and play it and play it, because I know it's the only thing I like to do, and the only shot I've got at not having to work at something I don't. The rush hour traffic on the Mancunian Way plays its weekday dirge, but I put it out of my mind, like I tried to do with the clock on the sausage factory wall.

I've got a gig at Night and Day tomorrow, and two new songs to add to the set. I don't know if anyone will ever pay me for making music, but I do know that apart from a few minutes every fortnight, I'm free. Maybe I'm selfish, or maybe it's because I've never fallen in love, but I'm glad I don't have to pay a mortgage on a house filled with furniture, and a picture on top of the TV of my dad, rampaging towards the opposition goal.

WHY DO YOU COME HERE?

John was unemployed, and put his M.A. in English Literature to use by lying on the couch all day and reading novels. He once thought of teaching English, but had come to realize that telling people what to do wasn't something he'd be good at. He didn't have a girlfriend, or many male friends, and spent a lot of time on his own.

One day he was looking through a brochure for a literature festival in Manchester, and saw a black and white photograph of a beautiful female novelist. She had pigtails and looked a bit like Betty Boop. John saw that she was doing a reading that afternoon, just across the road at Manchester Metropolitan University.

Last to perform, she was faultless. John was bewitched, and at home he read the story again. When he finished it he went back to see if she was still there, but the lights were off and the doors were locked.

The following day he went to Waterstone's and bought her first novel, even though he could barely afford it, and when he got home, read it in one sitting. The novel seemed to be autobiographical, and when John read some of Betty's interviews on the web and pieced them together with descriptions from the book, he figured out where she'd worked as a barmaid.

It was an American-style dive, where losers could rest their elbows in spilt beer and be guaranteed anonymity by the indifferent barmaids. John sat among them, and guessed that the

woman who served him was the basis for one of Betty's characters. On his way back from the toilets he saw her taking empties
out to the skip. She looked like Elizabeth Taylor in *Cat on a Hot
Tin Roof*, and when John mentioned Betty's book to her she
smiled shyly and asked him if he was a stalker.

Whenever John thought about Betty and Elizabeth he
couldn't help attributing them to the characters in Betty's book.
He also realized that whereas Betty had once been a barmaid—
serving, collecting empties, sweeping up broken glass—and had
now become a published novelist, Elizabeth still worked behind
the same bar.

He even had a couple of dreams about Elizabeth. In one he
turned a corner and saw her walking towards him in tears. In
the other they worked together, and met on the way in. She
smiled ruefully and said she had a hangover. Later in the dream
she sat on a desk facing him, and he put his hands on her hips.

John resumed his own writing. He'd had several poems published in small magazines, but after reading Betty's book he
thought he'd give prose a try. He also needed money, and knew
that nobody has ever made any money from poetry. Once John
had to go for an HIV test after spending the night with a Korean
hooker (this was when he was still drinking heavily). It had been
a stressful time, but also significantly interesting enough for
him to use it as the basis of a story. He wrote it in a couple of
hours and posted it to a national magazine, and after about six
months they wrote back and said it would be published a year
after that. Though he was pleased by the success, and glad of
the thirty quid he got for it, John was dismayed by the length of
time it took to get a story published.

He kept going to readings though, and at one of them saw
Betty. At the end of the night he went up to her and gave her a
poem that he'd written, something that he'd been carrying
around for months on the off-chance of meeting her. Though
she described the poem as being 'pretty concrete', John hoped
she was quietly flattered by it, and was glad of being able to
show her some gratitude.

John had been unemployed for a year and a half, and after an
ill-fated attempt to do some work overseas (for two days he tried
to teach on a building site in Hokkaido, spending the nights in

a run-down hotel filled with prostitutes and pimps), he signed-up for a creative writing course at Manchester University. As a result, he was able to get a loan from the bank.

Betty had started the same course, only to leave after signing a fifty grand publishing deal, and though John couldn't contemplate ever being paid that much, he felt sure that he had a novel inside him. He was excited at the prospect, and keen to meet fifteen other people who liked to read novels and tried to write.

Unfortunately for John, though he learned a lot from his tutors, he didn't really get on with his fellow students. They formed a clique that struck him as the antithesis of individuality, confirming all the reservations he'd had about creative writing courses. Another reason he didn't get on with his fellow students was because they betrayed a childish envy of Betty, and were unable to see beyond her physical beauty to the literary beauty of her sentences. He couldn't begin to respect them if they couldn't see how good she was. One week the American writer Jayne Anne Phillips took a short story workshop, and couldn't get a word in edgeways.

John wrote an autobiographical novel and passed the course. He felt that his writing had improved, and tried not to think about debts. He signed on the dole again and continued to read novels every day.

Betty's novel had received critical praise, and when her second came out it was similarly well received. She embarked on a tour around the country, and John got a ticket for a reading in Manchester. As usual, she read beautifully, charming the audience with her similes and her smiles, and afterwards John waited in line for an autograph. When she signed his book she remembered his face and frowned a little before smiling. He was as beguiled as ever and once again, when he read the book, he couldn't separate Betty from her protagonist.

John continued to go drinking in the American-style dive bar, and was amazed to see that Betty had begun to work there again. One night, when he caught her eye to ask for a drink, she came over.

'Hi. I love your second novel. How come you're back here?' John said.

'I'm just working the odd shift, for the money,' she answered.

'I didn't think you'd have to work now you're a writer.'

'That's a bit naïve. My money's running out, and anyway, I like working here.'

'Not according to your books you don't.'

'Yeah, well. That's fiction.'

'Oh, yeah. I know that. It's pretty autobiographical though, isn't it.'

'Some of it, yes.'

'What about . . .'

'Sorry,' she said, moving off to serve.

John carried on drinking, sipping from his bottle of beer and watching Betty behind the bar. She'd been nice to him at first, but now she'd begun to ignore him. He realized he was turning into one of the losers that populated her novels, so he struggled off the stool, conscious of his legs, and weaved his way home.

The following day John thought that Betty was different when she got behind the bar, that she put on a hard face and a curt disposition that fitted the role of an old barmaid rather than a young novelist. He had to read her first book again to remind himself of how beautiful she was.

Because the literature scene in Manchester was so small, John would often see Betty at readings and meet other people who knew her. Sometimes Betty smiled at him and asked him how he was, and he thought she was being friendly rather than kind. It was driving him mad, seeing her but not being able to get beyond the water-tread of acquaintance, and he began to regret his fawning.

He'd read an interview where she said that she did a lot of writing in the Central Library, so he started going there, and sure enough began to see her, usually on the way in or out, her beauty in microcosm between a woolly hat and a smothering of scarves.

John's own writing had stalled because he couldn't envisage being able to write as well as Betty, and certainly not as well as the great novelists of the past he read every day. Lost inside the four corners of his room, sometimes he wouldn't talk to anyone for days. He started drinking alone, and then got a letter from the DSS, threatening to stop his benefits.

Back in the American-style dive bar, John sipped from his bottle and watched Betty and Elizabeth serving. When he'd asked for a drink he noticed that Elizabeth was being a bit off-hand, not acknowledging him as the regular he'd become. Betty was the same, and when he tried to engage her in conversation she just walked away and busied herself with something or somebody else.

A bottle before closing time, John saw Betty go up to the DJ, and noticed them laughing together. John continued to drink, but then started to hear a pattern developing in the lyrics to different songs:

Why do you come here, why do you hang around?
What was it you wanted, tell me again so I know
Idiot wind, blowing every time you move your mouth

He wondered if he was being paranoid, and then he wondered if Betty was being paranoid. He continued to drink and didn't notice that the clock had gone two when the bouncer asked him to leave. By now, John was slurring his words, and as Betty passed with some empties, he tried to grab her arm. She shrugged him off, went back behind the bar and took away his unfinished bottle. He stared at her when she did it, and she stared right back.

'I've not, it's not . . .'

'Fuck off! Right? Just fuck off! LEAVE ME ALONE!' she shouted.

As the bouncer dragged him out, John banged his knees on the pavement, the impact leaving white marks on his jeans. He walked slowly through town, past red and yellow and blue cranes that rose high into the black sky. Under a railway bridge, he looked around for cameras and pissed all over his own shoes.

In the morning, he shuffled to the bathroom and filled a pint pot with water. Then he went into the living room and picked up a book that was resting on the arm of a chair. He threw it at the wall, and went across and shook the bookcase until the novels began to fall. When the shelves were empty, he started kicking it. Wood and splinters went everywhere, and when he finally stopped, he picked up all the bits of wood, went out onto the balcony, and threw them over the edge.

He stared at the rooftops of the city, and imagined all the people working in offices and warehouses and factories and shops. When he went back in he looked at the books scattered across the floor. Though it seemed a far less pleasurable alternative, he knew he was going to have to go out into the world and leave all that reading behind.

BROKEN DOLL

They were sitting on cardboard boxes next to the navy blue container, Brian and Mark in the shade of the heavy metal door, and Dave topless in the sun that slid down off the roof of the mill. On the other side of the car park, outside the entrance, three women in office clothes stood smoking cigarettes and sipping coffee from plastic cups.

'I'd give it that blonde,' said Mark.

'Yeah, me too. Jesus, look at that,' said Brian, as one of the women leaned over to put a cup on the floor.

'Just imagine getting her in the container,' said Mark.

'Yeah, you'd sweat your balls off,' said Brian.

'You sad bastards,' said Dave.

'Oh, so you're awake then?' said Brian.

'Shut up, fat boy. When was the last time you even saw yours?'

'Fuck off.'

'Oh, stop moaning will you. Look, we've got it cushy here, so don't complain.'

'I'm smoking too much Bob Hope. Was wasted again last night,' said Mark.

'Why do you bother?' said Brian.

'Same reason anyone does. Bet you had a few beers last night.'

'Yeah, but that's legal, mate. Hey, Dave, you're the student, what do you think?' said Brian.

'I don't give a shit, mate.'

'Nice to know education isn't going to waste,' said Mark.

'Listen, mate, it's a cushy number being a student, just like this job. There's plenty of people out there rushing around, stressed out, seizing the day, all that bollocks. Carpe diem— never was something more misappropriated.'

'What? Carp what?'

'*Carpe diem*, it's Latin for seize the day.'

'Thought you were on about fishing.'

'Seize the day, that means make the most of the day, not necessarily live for the moment. Go for it, yeah, let's all go for it, Thatcher's enduring dream, all out for number one, fuck anyone else, fuck society, get out of my way while I make my million. Then what will they spend it on? They'll just get ripped off, pay more for things than they should, waste what they've got, probably end up doing lines of coke off the bell end of an asylum seeker they got in to do the cleaning.'

'I think it's you wants to chill out,' said Brian, horizontal across four boxes.

'Oh, go back to sleep, big lad.'

'Shall we just take the trolleys back up? By the time we've been up there and washed-up it will be time for lunch anyway,' said Mark.

'Balls to it,' said Dave, flipping Brian off the boxes and onto the car park floor.

The flatbed trolleys were like the ones for baggage at airports. Picking up speed down the ramp that led past the goods entrance, they rolled them down to the lift doors before getting in the same way every time: Mark and Dave first, and then Brian squeezing in sideways, just able to turn and shut the doors behind him. Once up to the seventh floor they unlocked the heavy sliding door and went into the unit. Across the dusty floorboards, boxes were lined in rows like gravestones.

Mark went off to wash his hands, while Dave and Brian occupied their usual lunch time places, Dave in a big square armchair shaped from the boxes, and Brian on the deckchair he'd brought from home. Brian switched on the radio and then filled his French bread with slices of salami, while Dave opened a newspaper.

'You scruffy lot, I don't know how you can eat without

washing your hands. All the shit on them boxes, and now look at you, holding that bread,' said Mark, sitting on the edge of a flatbed and delving into a carrier bag.

After they'd eaten, Mark and Dave got up and began kicking a football, while Brian remained eating. Soon they started aiming shots towards Brian, sometimes missing by a distance and sometimes getting quite close, until eventually Mark pinged him on the back of the head, sending coke flying up out of the bottle and the French stick crumbling in a clenched hand.

'You arseholes,' said Brian.

They always had two hours for lunch, and when that time was up they loaded the flatbeds with boxes, wheeled them out of the unit, locked the metal sliding door behind them and went down in the lift to put more boxes in the container.

Brian walked like his pants were round his ankles, and soon the back of his shirt was dark with sweat. Mark held the boxes out with his arms rather than dirty the front of his City shirt, while Dave often struggled to lift them, groaning every time he picked one up or put one down, dust staining his stomach like a botched tattoo.

After working for about half an hour they had another break, all of them sitting on boxes in the shadow of the container. Mark lit a fag, Brian slumped back on his box, and Dave hunched forward, gripping slices of his beer belly, lifting and dropping the slack flesh like a man provoking bubbles in a bath.

'Must be more to life than this,' said Mark.

'No,' said Brian.

'Are you out tonight, Brian? Hitting the town?' said Dave.

'No . . . I don't think so. I'll just stay in with my girlfriend and watch the TV.'

'Rock n' roll, eh?' said Dave.

'What about you, donkey dick?' said Mark.

'Yeah, might do. I need a drink to face the prospect of coming here every day,' said Dave.

'Listen, you're free in a bit. Back to Uni. We're here for life, mate,' said Mark.

'Why don't you do something else then? You're too bright to just be doing this all day,' said Dave.

'Piss easy, isn't it? No hassle, decent wonga—piece of piss. All right, so it's boring as fuck, but you can't have everything,' said Mark.

'Yeah, but don't you want to do anything with your life?'

'Listen to him, eh, Brian. Look, getting a degree's not going to get you anywhere. Every fucker's got one these days.'

'Got more chance than you have.'

'What is it you're doing, History? What the fuck use is that? My old fella told me that subjects like History and Geography are only good for answering questions on Trivial Pursuit.'

'It's important, mate, especially in this world of bullshit information. I'm learning about all the shit that's happened. Did you know twice as many people died in the First World War than the second? Scary shit like that, or that millions died in the Russian gulags, and some bit their own hands off so they could get out of working in the snow.'

'Bit their own hands off? Fuck off,' said Brian.

'It's true, fat boy. Stuff like that happens, and it's people like you who watch TV and eat happy meals and play with your dick in the bath and don't know fuck all who make this world what it is.'

'Alright. You're boring the arse off me now.'

'Go back to sleep, big lad,' said Mark, stamping out his fag.

'Hey up, here she is. Look at them,' said Brian, squinting through the sunlight at the group of women who'd come outside to smoke. 'Makes me horny as fuck, this weather.'

A breeze moved through the car park and caused trees to sway like drunks by the riverside. Beneath the trees, a rabbit bobbed through the grass as though it were being continually kicked in the arse.

'God, it's fucking boiling. I'm grinding rocks today,' said Brian.

'Thanks for that, Brian,' said Dave.

'Listen, why don't we go down to the river and have a swim?' said Mark.

'Nah, I can't be arsed,' said Brian.

'Yeah, I'm up for it,' said Dave, 'You stay here, fat lad.'

Mark and Dave made their way across the car park and squeezed between two parked lorries and into the undergrowth beneath the trees. They stumbled towards the river's edge and saw a five feet drop to the water. After wading through brambles looking for an easier way in, their legs became scratched and dirty. As Mark squinted through the trees at Brian slumped on his back outside the container, Dave kicked at what he thought was a broken doll.

~

The man that the police charged had first been suspected when a woman contacted them about photographs of young girls she'd seen on his mobile. At first she hadn't said anything, but then she read a book about the murder of two schoolgirls by a caretaker, and how the girlfriend had been implicated.

One of his jobs was to mow the playing fields and trim the trees of the local primary school, and he'd sit in the van with his workmates afterwards, drinking from his flask of coffee and watching the playground. One day he noticed a young girl in a bright red anorak, whose long blond hair bounced up and down as she ran and, almost immediately, he got out of the van and busied himself tidying the load of broken branches.

When they knocked off work early and he'd dropped his workmates off, he drove around the perimeter of the fields, and when he saw her again in a flash of red and yellow, poking a stick out through the railings, he snatched a quick photo with his phone.

He began to go every Friday, and once did what he'd only ever done before over pictures. For a month afterward he didn't go back, but one day, when his hay fever was bad and tears filling his eyes gave an added glisten to the sun, he watched her playing with her friends in the furthest corner of the field. He went over to the railings, and when the ball they were playing with bounced towards him, she ran to within yards, smiling.

After her mum came to take Elesse home, he followed them. In the evenings he'd drive to the estate and walk his dog in the hope of seeing her, and one night she was sitting with a friend on swings in the park. When he passed them on the street a few minutes later, she smiled down at his dog and then up at him. He almost grabbed her then, but didn't, and it was only when he saw her by herself a week later that he hit her on the back of the head with a rock.

∾

As they sat watching the fixed images that lined the familiar route, neither of them spoke, instead letting the lilting voice of the Irish DJ wash over them like the smiles of neighbours, most of whom didn't know what to say and so didn't say anything. On the dual carriageway, beneath a billboard that twisted and turned to reveal different gaudy coloured slogans and images, a bunch of flowers wrapped around a lamppost faded and grew smaller with every passing day, until all that was left were withered stems and rain-lashed plastic.

The washed-out green hills above the cemetery revealed the rushing approach of a sunlight that within seconds filled the grounds. As they knelt down before their daughter's grave and replaced the day-old flowers, Karen scraped bird droppings from the headstone. She talked as though Elesse could hear her, and Richard tensed his hands in his trouser pockets, the fingernails that dug into his palms somehow stopping him from falling.

Though Richard began to go less and less, Karen still went to the cemetery every Saturday and, before catching the bus, always bought flowers from the same sad-eyed florist; a man with the sympathetic countenance of a pallbearer, a man she guessed knew sorrows at least the equal of hers. In the cemetery itself, she saw others like her, weekend pilgrims to the sight of a lifetime's grief, walking with heads bowed, their loosely gripped flowers trailing behind them between rows and rows of stone.

∾

Back at the mill, Mark, Dave and Brian read the newspapers and talked about what they'd seen on the news. From the window next to the lift they could see right down to the river, and following its silver slant, see the area of undergrowth where the police and forensics had crawled.

A man walked his dog just yards from where the black and yellow tape had cordoned off the crime scene, and above him a cloud hid the sun briefly then moved across the skyline in a barely-heard collusion of wind.

For their lunch break, Mark, Dave and Brian had gone out to sit on the top of the fire escape, at the side of the building shaded from the sun and out of sight of the crime scene. From this new vantage point they could see the gates to the car park of the mill, and the porter's lodge where wagons stopped in a squash of brakes. Beyond the lodge the view expanded for miles, over terraced houses, schools, churches, and a strip of motorway with cars moving in line like models dragged by string.

'Beautiful on here, boys,' said Brian.

'Yeah, I suppose so,' said Mark.

'You won't get a tan though, Brian,' said Dave.

'I'm not bothered about that,' said Brian.

Mark had walked down a few steps and sat beneath Dave and Brian, looking towards the car park at a woman in a low cut blouse bending over to put something in the boot of her car. He took a long drag on his joint and hugged a knee up to his chest, then let his head fall back before blowing smoke out above himself.

The wind began to get up. From their exposed seats Dave and Brian struggled to control the newspapers they read, until eventually Dave's escaped from him altogether and flew out sideways from the fire escape rail, spiralling down onto the roof of the porter's lodge where the red lettering of the paper's name was still visible, but not the headlines beneath.

THE FRESHER

With his head sticking out from beneath the pushed-up window, Darren watched his dad's car move slowly across the car park of the halls of residence and indicate left before disappearing back to Manchester.

He pulled down the window and looked around at the room that would be his for the duration of the academic year. It smelled of the empty wardrobe in the corner and also contained a bed, with its wooden base and not-quite-new mattress, a desk, complete with knifed-on graffiti, a shin-high coffee table, and a metal bin, lined with a black bag that overlapped the rim like the folded-up sleeve of a shiny black shirt. The dull white walls were dotted with old clouds of blue-tack, and other bits where when it had been pulled off it had left grey shadows. Darren sat down on the mattress and looked at his suitcase and the cardboard boxes that contained all he'd chosen to bring. He gazed through the window at his view: the car park leading to the main road busy with traffic and, beyond, a park with bare black trees and a wino holding a plastic bottle and leaning on one end of a bench as though trying to tip it up.

After fifteen minutes of unpacking he put the kettle on and made a cup of tea. Lying back on the bed he sipped from the cup and listened as someone with a very loud voice arrived in the room next door, talking excitedly to his parents. When he'd finished his tea, Darren looked through the stuff that had been left on the bed to welcome him—the fan of flyers, the itinerary for Freshers' Week, the rules and regulations for the halls. He picked up his course handbook, made a mental note of where to register, and then lay back on the bed to read *Silas Marner*, the first book on the 19th Century Literature module. Halfway down the first page, the bass from the stereo next door almost shook the book from his hands. He got up and put on his coat.

After ten minutes he'd reached the centre of town, and then five minutes later had passed through it. Rising above it all was the big blue transporter bridge, as seen on the cover of the prospectus. When he got to it, Darren went on and, standing beside a couple of cars, looked up as they were carried across the river to the other side. Standing by the river, Darren watched as the bridge wheeled around, the turning arm hundreds of feet above like a slow sarcastic indicator of the whole surrounding area.

Making his way back through town, Darren stopped off at Kwik Save. He got back to the halls, showed his ID card to the porter and walked through the communal kitchen back to his room, where he put the milk and butter on the window ledge and everything else—bread, jam, tins, on one side of the desk. The room next door had gone quiet and, relaxed in the relative silence, Darren ate a tin of fruit cocktail and finally started on *Silas Marner*, which he read in its entirety before falling asleep.

The TV room was usually populated by students slumped before the goggle box as a respite from the task of spending all of their loans before Christmas, and Darren soon realized that the only time he could be guaranteed to predict what they were watching was when there was a big match on.

One Wednesday night, when he was sure that most of them would be out on the regular student night, *Romp*, he was surprised to find a handful of students still in the TV room. From what he could gather, there were three American women, an Italian bloke with a Spanish friend, also male, and a fat Welsh lad dozing over a can of lager. Darren noticed that one of the American women was reading a book by Alice Walker.

'Have you read *The Color Purple*?' he asked.

'Err, yes. Have you ?' she answered.

'No, I've seen the film though.'

'Oh, right,' she said, before looking back down at her book.

At the end of the film, Darren put his four empties in the metal bin and made his way back upstairs, hoping to get some sleep before his neighbour returned in the small hours.

Darren bumped into the American girl again a few days later, and when they chatted they found out that they were doing different modules on the same English course. She asked him what room he was in and said she'd pop down and visit him some time.

When she put a note under Darren's door he jumped off the bed to read it. The note Melanie had written told him her room number, said that he was welcome to visit, and also said that *Life is life, not mood*, a quotation attributed to Alice Walker.

As he stood outside Melanie's room, Darren checked his hair in the mirror above the sink. He could smell incense coming from inside the room. When he knocked on the door there was no answer. He knocked again and there was still no response, so he began to slowly open the door, at which point Melanie appeared, headphones lodged in her ears and what Darren recognized as the faint strained melodies of *American Beauty*.

'Hi, hi, come in!' she shouted.

'Hi,' said Darren, before looking around for somewhere to sit.

The room was full of books and there were incense candles smoking in the corner. There was a globe on the desk and a map on the wall with a big circle around what seemed like an outsized splodge of the USA. On the opposite wall there were posters of Hilary Clinton, Maya Angelou, The Grateful Dead and Brad Pitt.

'Take a seat,' she said, taking a pile of thick woolly jumpers off the only chair. 'I'm making some coffee, you want some?'

'No thanks, I don't really drink coffee.'

'You don't drink coffee? My god, I don't think I could *live* without it.'

She picked up the kettle and went outside to the sink to fill it before plugging it back in and spooning coffee and sugar into the cup.

'So, you got my note?'

'Yeah.'

'What did you think when you saw it? Did you think I was just some crazy American?'

'Well, at first, yes,' he said, 'I'm joking.'

'Oh, right. I'm still getting used to what you call humour over here.'

'No, really, at first I was a bit annoyed to be honest, but then I thought that it's probably one of the nicest things anyone has ever done for me.'

'Really?'

'Yeah.'

'So, what are you reading at the moment?'

'Err . . . Dylan Thomas.'

'I love Dylan Thomas. Have you read him before?'

'No.'

'No? We read him a few years ago. Welsh, right? Yeah, he's cool, you read that one, *In The White Giants Thigh*? It's my favourite, I guess.'

'I find it a bit difficult to be honest, I don't really like poetry that much.'

'Hey, you know, if you want you can bring it up here and we can drink coffee and read our books and then ask each other what we think.'

'Yeah, okay.'

'You want to get it now?'

'Okay.'

On his way back into Melanie's room he looked at himself in the mirror again.

'Won't you have a coffee?' she asked.

'Okay then,' he said.

As they sat there together, Melanie at the head of her bed and Darren on the chair, he noticed that she was reading a book about Shakespeare called *The Invention of the Human*. 'That looks pretty difficult,' he said.

'This? No. The thing is you're only in your first semester, I'm in my final year, so I'm bound to be a little ahead of you in my reading. Anyway, just be quiet for a while, okay? Then we can talk later.'

'Okay,' he said, looking back down at the Dylan Thomas, unable to concentrate on any one of the images that tumbled towards him like bright and brilliant children.

'Listen,' she said, after a few minutes, 'maybe we should go out for coffee tomorrow.'

'Yeah, or for a drink?'

'I don't drink, honey.'

'You don't drink?'

'Is that so incredible?'

'No, no.'

The next night they went to a coffee shop and listened to the performance poets on stage. The men read about sex, and the women read about cats, and all were nervous before the microphone. 'You should see some of the readings in New York, Darren. Better than this,' said Melanie, as the last reader came off stage.

'Wouldn't be hard.'

'Hey, it takes a lot to get up there. I don't see you doing it.'

'I've no interest in doing it, thanks. I've no interest in inflicting my insecurities on anyone else.'

'Except me, right?'

'Well, only if you'll listen.'

'I'm all ears, honey.'

'I like that, 'honey', it makes you sound like a cowgirl.'

'You should see me riding.'

'I'd love to.'

'Hey, take it easy. I didn't mean like that.'

Walking back down the main road that led to the halls of residence, they passed pubs and pizza shops, closed cafés and estate agents, and weaved in and out of rubbish that littered the wind-blown streets like lost tickets.

'I wonder why I came here, you know?' said Darren.

'Yeah, me too,' Melanie answered, before reaching down to hold his hand.

Back at the halls Melanie walked up the stairs behind Darren, and when they reached his floor she asked him to come up in ten minutes. When he did so, he went through the unlocked door into the darkness and climbed into the single bed, his arm brushing across her nipples as he reached across to hold her.

Later she said that neither of them would get any sleep if they spent the whole night together, so he got up, put on his t-shirt and trousers, and carried his shoes down the fire escape stairs. Lying in his room, the moonlight through the cheap curtains colouring everything blue, he resisted the temptation to get up and slam the door when he heard his neighbour's snoring.

Darren didn't get up until about four the following afternoon and, after getting dressed and having a shave, he went down to the canteen for a subsidised evening meal. Sitting by the window, he pushed his tray away and leant his arms on the table. Sipping from his orange juice he looked outside and saw Melanie walking into the halls alongside another man. Darren got up and carried his tray to the hatch, where the dinner lady smiled and thanked him for bringing it back. When the student behind him put a tray down she said the same thing again.

When he eventually walked up the fire escape stairs, planning to knock on Melanie's door, he stopped to check himself in the mirror and heard the deep timbre of one half of a conversation inside. Unheard, he turned around and went back down the fire escape stairs. Between her room and his, he fell short of breath as he repeatedly kicked the banister.

In one of his seminars, Darren discussed the poetry of Dylan Thomas with one of his fellow students, a mature student of seventy-three years of age called Eddie, a Scouser with a florid, bald head and a beard like Leo Tolstoy, and they went out for a pint together afterwards.

'Anniversary today, our kid,' said Eddie, sipping from his Guinness.

'What of?'

'The wife.'

'Oh, right.'

'No point me buying her anything, though.'

'Why not?'

'Well, she's brown bread.'

'Oh, sorry, Eddie.'

'It's alright, don't you worry, our kid. You weren't to know. Fifteen years to the day. Breast cancer.'

'Sorry, mate.'

'I don't often talk about her. You know, I remember the first time I saw her, working at Littlewoods in the town centre, smiling at customers and bossing everyone around, ha, ha, that was my Lillian.'

'She sounds like a nice lady.'

'The nicest—Bootle's finest. I proposed to her on the day of the cup final, when we beat the Geordies. She never liked football.'

'How long were you married for?'

'Fifteen years, I've been as long without now. Though it took me long enough to find her, because I was married before, you know. Sheila. She was an ugly woman—hard too. I only ever hit her in self-defence. That's a joke. Don't ever marry an ugly woman, though, it takes the life right out of you.'

'I'll try and remember.'

'Joke was it was her that was playing away in the end. Good of her, though. She wasn't a patch on Lillian. You know, I don't remember anything about marrying Sheila, but I remember everything about me and Lillian. Waiting outside the church, the leaves flying off the trees, wondering if she was coming, which was stupid, but you know, when you're standing there in your best gear and all your pals are saying that the bride's always late, you pretend to laugh, but I remember how nervous I was getting, and I started to think about those poor scallies that you read about getting left alone at the altar, I mean I don't know how you'd get over that, but yeah, when she turned up, in a silver Merc it was, I couldn't really see in the window, but when she got out and the sun fell across the white dress and she looked for me in the crowd, I remember how that smile of hers, God, what a smile it was, I remember how she looked right at me and all my nerves just went away, and when I turned around and went in the church it felt like I was having a dream or something, you know, and I don't remember the vows really, except for people laughing at my middle name . . .'

' . . . What is it?'

'It doesn't matter.'

'No, go on, what is it?'

'Primrose.'

'Pri . . . (cough) that's not so bad.'

'Well, it got a laugh. I don't know. Anyway, when I kissed her after the vows I forgot all about them, forgot anyone else was there, and the vicar had to have a quiet word, I'll always remember that, the sarky old get. And we walked out of there and went straight into the Merc and off on our honeymoon to New Brighton. It was the best day of my life, our kid, and I've buried her now. But, my God, she was so beautiful it made my stomach ache to look at her. She was like something out of a poem. Anyway, remember, our kid, like I said, don't ever marry an ugly woman. Find one that's beautiful and you'll stroll through life easy, well, you do have your troubles, like anyone else, but it just doesn't ever seem so bad.'

'She sounds like a great woman, Eddie.'

'She was.'

After they left the pub, Eddie got a taxi home and Darren walked back to the halls. When he got in he switched on the lamp and looked out of the window as his neighbour went past with two other lads. Behind them, Melanie followed with three other girls, her high heels clattering.

THE FACES

Jo and Jackie were both in a band that gigged around Manchester. They played regularly at Night and Day, the Roadhouse, the Retro Bar, Jabez Clegg, Joshua Brooks, the Star and Garter, the Tiger Lounge and most of the other small gig venues in the town. Recently they'd had a profile in a local listings magazine, and were putting the finishing touches to an E.P.

One Saturday afternoon they were both watching the TV. It was the day of George Best's funeral in Northern Ireland, and it was raining there too. 'God, I didn't know he was that popular,' said Jackie.

'He must have been. He was a good-looking bloke. I think there's a bit of that Diana scenario too, the sharing of public grief.'

'I don't really understand it. People die every day, people equally important, but thousands don't go to their funerals.'

'But he was the best footballer that ever played the game. That's why they're all standing in the rain. They showed some clips before and he looked pretty good. Shame he grew that beard. You should watch, it might improve your football skills.'

'What are you trying to say? It's not like you've ever come along to watch me play. Anyway, Pele was better.'

'Well, you've got enough of a fan club already. Jenny and her mates drool over you every game.'

'Oh shut up, Jo. How would you know if you never turn up?'

'I've been told.'

As Jackie went to her room, Jo watched hundreds of black umbrellas shining like beads along the road to Stormont. Above them, a black statue pointed a finger in the rain.

Jo worked in the Central Library cafe. She did a thirty-five hour week and wanted all the overtime she could get. One of the benefits of working there was that she could take home any food that was left at the end of the day. If friends came in she could let them have stuff without paying, and a lot of her musician friends turned up at various times for a handout.

Adrian played the bass in a local band, and Jo knew him well. The Manchester music scene was kept alive by local bands that watched each other, and it was a clique that most enjoyed. Adrian cut an amusingly bedraggled figure, his black beard sticking out like a trampled bush.

'Hi. Just these sandwiches and a coffee please,' said Adrian.

'Sure you don't want anything else? Something to take with you, maybe?' said Jo.

'No, no, this'll do me thanks.'

A group of pensioners left the theatre in slow motion as Adrian ripped the cover from his shrink-wrapped sandwiches. When it was time for her break, Jo came over, and Adrian smiled as she took the wrapper off a teacake.

'Skiving again, eh?' he said.

'Well, no, I'll just give it five minutes. It's always mad when a play's finished.'

'Yeah. No, I'm joking anyway. You work too hard as it is. I wonder how you can write songs after working in here all day.'

'Well, you know, the more I do the more I can do. You just get used to it. Anyway, what've you been up to?'

'I've just been in the library this morning. It's warmer than my flat.'

'I didn't know you could read,' said Jo, pointing to Adrian's rucksack. 'Let's have a look then.'

'Okay, but there's nothing really interesting.'

He opened the bag and took out a batch of novels.

'Turgenev, Chekhov, Dostoyevsky, Solzhenitsyn. Bit of light reading, eh?'

'I'm just getting into them. I read *Crime and Punishment* and loved it.'

'Yeah, *The Brothers Karamazov* is even better.'

'You've read it then, have you?'

'Yeah, I did my degree in Russian.'

'Really? Wow.'

'Pushkin is my favourite. *Eugene Onegin*. The Russians love Pushkin.'

'Right. I've been getting into Chekhov. You ever read *The Lady with the Dog*?'

'No. I'm not that keen on short stories really, but Dostoyevsky's good, and *The First Circle*.'

'Yeah, I like the library. It's great for a man with no money. I get the books for free and you feed me up too.'

'I'd never have guessed you liked Russian novels. Mind you, you look a bit like a serf.'

'Ha, cheers. You know what it's like when you're in a band. All people want to talk about is the gig. Some of us are into other stuff.'

'I know what you mean.'

'Anyway, talking of which, are you and Jackie coming down to the Retro on Friday?'

'Err, well, I will be. I don't know about Jackie.'

'Alright, well, I'll probably see you in there then.'

'Yeah. Are you sure you don't want anything to take with you? They just throw all these sandwiches out.'

'No, I'm alright. It's a waste that. Can't they give them to the homeless or something?'

'No, the council won't do that. The homeless guys have to go through the bins at the back.'

'That's shit. Well, alright, cheers anyway, Jo. See you.'

'See you, Ade.'

Jackie was in the bath when Jo got home, and clothes dropped by the door looked like evidence of a seduction. Sitting on the couch and picking up the TV guide, Jo noticed that Jackie had circled *Bad Girls*.

In the kitchen, a pile of dishes rose from the sink and there was a pool of water at the base of the fridge, making channels between waves of lino. Jo opened the door and removed the spoiled food, then put on her coat and went out to the chippy.

When she came back, Jackie was drying her hair in front of the TV.

'I've bought you some chips,' said Jo.

'Why? We can't afford that.'

'Course we can. Didn't you notice the fridge?'

'Oh, yeah. I was going to tell you.'

'What are we going to do about it?'

'We'll have to wait until you get paid.'

'Oh, right. Until I get paid. What about you?'

'Well, you're the one who works. We agreed on that, didn't we? So I can stay home and practise piano.'

'Yeah, I suppose.'

'You know it makes sense. You know how important the piano and keyboard is.'

~

On Jackie's birthday, Jo organised a fancy dress party and invited some of their friends. Dave came as Elvis Presley, Katie, Kelly, Jenny and Sally as the Spice Girls, Helen as Humphrey Bogart, Terry as Marilyn Monroe, John as George Bush, Simon as Edmund Blackadder (Series 2 — comedy breasts episode), Nick as a Harlem Globetrotter and Colin as Tony Blair. Last to arrive was Adrian, who'd come dressed as a soldier.

After a couple of buckets of mulled wine had been emptied, the party began to liven up. Elvis Presley snogged Posh Spice (Sally), watched by Elizabeth 1st (Jo) and the wicked witch (Jackie). George Bush and Tony Blair slipped from serious discussion to mocking laughter and back again. Humphrey Bogart stood silently in the corner, casting brooding glances across the room towards Marlin Monroe, who seemed unperturbed by the Harlem Globetrotter spinning a basketball in her face. Edmund Blackadder just sat at the table, making sarcastic comments about the wine.

Jo noticed that Adrian wasn't around and found him sitting by himself in the bedroom, reading Pushkin's *The Queen of Spades*.

'So, this is where you've sneaked to, is it?'

'Looks that way.'

'Are you alright?'

'Yeah, I just don't really like parties. I don't know why I came.'

'Yeah, well, Jackie wanted it, she likes to be the centre of attention.'

'Yeah.'

'I organized all this, got the food from work, made the mulled wine. She hasn't thanked me or anything.'

'Well . . . I hope you don't mind me asking, but are you two getting on okay?'

' . . . I think so. What makes you say that?'

'Oh, no reason. Hey, this is a cool story.'

'I know. Anyway, I'm going back in there. Feel free to come and join in,' said Jo, before kissing Adrian on the cheek and going back into the living room.

'Where have you been?' said Jackie.

'I was just looking for Adrian, that's all.'

'What's he doing in our room?'

'Reading a book.'

'Reading a book? Wow, party animal.'

'I know,' said Jo, scooping wine from the bucket.

Jackie had been in charge of the CD player, but in the small hours Tony Blair suggested they have a jam, so the instruments came out and everyone else watched as Blair and Bush traded guitar riffs. Eventually only Jo, Jackie and Adrian remained, and they sat together on the couch as an orange sunrise filled the room.

'I'm going to bed anyway. You coming, Jo? Adrian can let himself out,' said Jackie.

'No, not yet. I'm just going to tidy up a bit.'

'Whatever. You can always crash on the couch, Adrian.'

'Thanks.'

Jo began to tidy the table, picking up all the paper plates and the plastic cups and emptying them into a bin bag. Adrian offered to help, but Jo said it was okay. When she went to the kitchen, he followed her in, and as she stood at the sink, he put his arms around her waist.

'What are you doing?'

'Nothing'

'Jackie will hear us.'

'Don't worry,' said Adrian, turning her around and cupping her face in his hands.

∼

Jo and Adrian began to see each other at least once a week, usually after Jo had finished work. Adrian would wait at the staff entrance at the back of the Central Library, and they'd cross Albert Square and go for a drink in the Town Hall Tavern.

One night, Dave—who'd been a roadie for Jo and Jackie's band and gone to the party as Elvis—happened to bump into them in Albert Square. They didn't look the least bit worried that he'd seen them, and when they asked him to a gig, he went along.

The gig was at a bar called Timesis, on Lloyd Street. After getting a drink they sat on a leather couch and watched a man dressed in a gorilla suit switch on a drill suspended inside a wire cage. As the drill vibrated and swung around, the strange whirring and clanging was recorded on tape. The man in the gorilla suit then unplugged the drill and re-wound the tape so they could all listen again.

Jo and Adrian seemed amused by Dave's discomfort, laughing and smiling and looking into each other's eyes. The next act was a woman scraping a stick across a broken xylophone and shouting the poetry of Geoffrey Hill as though it were primal scream therapy.

Dave went to the bar again and came back with a bottle of beer each for Jo and Adrian, who were now sat closer together on the couch. A few more acts appeared, including a one-man band with cymbals strapped to his knees, and a man in a flying helmet and goggles playing reggae tunes on a tuba.

Though it was obvious to all concerned what was going on, nobody actually broached the subject of Jo and Adrian's getting together, and at the end of the night they both bid Dave goodbye as though nothing untoward or unusual had occurred all evening.

As Dave walked home down Oxford Road, he thought about Jackie. He'd got to know her quite well during his time as a roadie, and bemoaned his luck when he found out she was a lesbian.

When he asked her about it, in his blunt, working class way, she smiled and told him that she thought of herself as bisexual. She'd had boyfriends in the past but had fallen in love with Jo, who just happened to be a woman.

Dave didn't have a girlfriend himself, and he didn't know a great deal about relationships. To him they were just annoying aspects of soap operas in which everyone seemed to act the same way. It bothered him that people in real life also acted like that, and he didn't know which influenced which.

For a week and a half after going to the gig with Jo and Adrian, Dave lay awake at night, feeling the guilt of not telling Jackie. But one night, after having too much to drink, he sent her a text. She phoned him back almost immediately, and when he confirmed what he knew, she cried.

The next day Jo and Adrian turned up at Dave's. When he let them in they said nothing and just stared at him from on the couch.

'Look, Jo, I would have done exactly the same if it was you,' said Dave, breaking the silence.

'Look, Dave, don't try and get out of this,' said Jo.

'I'm not trying to get out of anything.'

'You grassed us up, Dave,' said Adrian.

'So what?'

'So fucking what?' said Adrian, rising from his chair and pushing Dave against the wall, only for Dave to bounce back and shove him to the floor.

'Look, I want to be able to sleep at night. That's the only fucking reason,' said Dave.

'Alright boys, don't be stupid. Look, Dave, just stay out of it, alright?' said Jo.

'I will, that's fine by me,' said Dave, and with that, they left.

When they'd had time to consider it, Jo and Adrian realized that Dave had saved them a difficult task, and though it's not how they would have liked things to happen, they soon forgot about him.

Meanwhile, Jackie met up with Dave for coffee, and Dave began to feel a degree of affection for her that he'd never known before. The fact that she'd been part of what Dave saw as a beautiful couple meant that he'd forgotten his initial attraction to her, and now he began to mistake his compassion for something different. The next time they met he told her she was beautiful. Perhaps if he'd been more subtle things may have happened between them, but his clumsy admission reminded Jackie of all the bashful boys she'd wasted time with at school.

Jo had kept in touch with Jackie, and they'd meet up, mainly so that Jo could feel better for seeing Jackie not crying. When Jo and Adrian moved in together, Jackie saw it as the end of any prospect of reconciliation and began to go clubbing on Canal Street.

Jo and Adrian continued to go to the Town Hall Tavern, and one night Jo said that she wasn't going to be drinking alcohol for a while. When Adrian found out why, he immediately got himself a pint.

'Jesus Christ, Jo. I thought you were taking care of it,' said Adrian.

'I was, I must have forgot.'

'Fucking hell. You don't sound too bothered.'

'I was just waiting for what your reaction would be.'

'Well, what did you expect? It's not like we've talked about it, is it?'

'No. You're right.'

After Adrian's reaction, Jo got really upset and called Jackie, and the news revived memories of conversations they'd had in the past. Adrian became increasingly jealous of Jackie, and soon he began to go out drinking on his own. He'd sit at the bar in Night and Day, ignoring the bands and the barmaids and succumbing blissfully to the thoughtlessness of drinking. Adrian and Jo gradually drifted apart, and after Jo had had the baby she moved back in with Jackie.

Not long after that, Dave saw Adrian sitting on his own in Night and Day, with his hands among a circle of empty bottles, and his eyes dazed and saddened by beer. Dave left without saying anything, but couldn't help wondering if the baby had always been destined for two mothers.

MARKED BY THE RINGING

I looked at the building beneath my window and remembered my surprise when I'd walked past the front door and read that it was the 'European Opera Centre'. It seemed like an exaggeration, but I'd come to enjoy the strains of singing that emerged like sashes pulled from a hat. Now a man on a cherry picker was boarding-up the windows.

In the evening I watched a reality TV show and after that I turned over to a programme about people who paid for their pets to be buried. As I sat there watching a man who travelled three hours a day to visit a dead dog, I thought about the presenter of the reality show, the most sanctimonious character I'd ever heard. When someone was evicted from the show, she criticized and made judgements about them with the benefit of twenty-twenty hindsight and the backing of a baying crowd. I wondered if she could see anything in the world beyond her craving for acceptance and popular appeal. Just because something reflected popular opinion, did that necessarily mean it was the truth?

A woman with sixteen cats was washing the black and white corpse of one of them, ready to put it into a pine box. When she did so, two men dressed in black placed the tiny coffin into the back of a hearse. A furnace opened and a man scraped out the ashes with a spade. Then the programme showed a service being read on a rain-lashed hillside, with a huddle of crying mourners and the owner of the cemetery holding an umbrella and puffing out his cheeks.

I'd been doubled-up laughing throughout most of the pro-gramme. I remembered the death of my own cat when I was a child, and how I hadn't felt much grief. The cat—a lovably can-tankerous, flea-bitten old beast—had become skinnier and skin-nier, and would dribble on my knees or tickle my hand with softened teeth. When he died I felt a sense of inevitability, and a warm melancholy that I kind of liked.

I flicked around the channels for something else to watch, but found nothing except the news. As I watched the mixture of tit-for-tat violence, horror and sadness, followed by the weath-er, I became aware of a smoke alarm going off in one of the flats. I muted the TV and listened. I was ready for bed, but I knew I'd never be able to sleep with the alarm ringing. I walked to the living room window and looked at parked cars that were all covered in snow. I went into the kitchen, rolled-up the blind and watched the streets at the front, where a black band of hooded kids on BMX bikes cycled in circles near a phone box.

The alarm was still ringing and I began to worry that there might actually be a fire. If that was the case then why hadn't somebody else sorted it out? Were they all deaf, or just so apa-thetic that they didn't care if the whole building burnt to the ground? I opened the front door and went out. As I leaned over the rail to try and work out exactly where the alarm was coming from, my legs felt the cold. It seemed as though the alarm was from upstairs. Why couldn't any of the neighbours hear it?

I thought of the face of the fireman who would ask why nobody had done anything. Even my imagination was making me feel guilty, so I got dressed and grudgingly went upstairs. Following the sound of the alarm to its source, I banged on the door of number 70. Nobody answered, but when I tried the han-dle, the door opened. I went in and stood directly beneath the alarm. The door to the living room was closed, and I had no idea what might be behind it. My mind flashed with images of a flaming body or a skeletal corpse, but when I opened the door all I could see was the back of a head and, in front of that, Jeremy Paxman. When I shouted, a thin old man rose from his seat and pointed at the alarm.

'Hi, mate, sorry for barging-in. I thought there was a fire or something,' I said.

The man just smiled and pointed.

'Is everything alright?'

'Can't turn it off.'

'There's no fire?'

The man walked into the kitchen and switched off the mains, sending the flat into a brief period of darkness, marked by the ringing.

'Won't go off.'

'Alright, mate. I just wanted to make sure there was no fire,' I said, beginning to feel anxious at having barged into a stranger's house.

'Must be the central heating or something,' said the man.

'Yeah, well, maybe open a window,' I said, moving out towards the front door.

'It'll go off in a bit.'

'Alright, mate. I just wanted to make sure you were alright,' I said, from the landing, as the old man slammed the door.

When I got in I went straight to bed, glad of the warmth, and wondered about the wisdom of suggesting the old man open some windows.

I tried reading my battered copy of *The Loved One*, but the alarm meant I couldn't concentrate. I kept thinking about the old man and said to myself that I'd done my bit. I didn't need to do that much. After all, no one else bothered; the old man could have burnt to death as far as they were concerned.

Switching off the bedside lamp, I put my head under the covers to reduce the noise. I couldn't sleep, and got up to look at my own smoke alarm. After switching it off at the mains, I squinted in the dark at the tiny white box. I'd always told myself that I wasn't mechanically minded, and knew no better way to account for the fact that I couldn't dismantle the alarm.

I remembered back to a time when I'd got my dad out from work to help me unscrew a car battery. I couldn't remove it, but when dad came back he just turned either side of the screw in opposite directions and looked at me with pity in his eyes.

I continued to push and prod at the alarm, fearful of breaking it. Then, as my eyes adjusted to the darkness, I saw an arrow on the box, pushed in that direction, and slid the cover off. I got dressed and went back upstairs, and walking through the door onto the landing, saw the old man.

'I'm going to phone the fire brigade,' he said.

'No listen, mate, I can try and take it down for you.'

'Alright.'

We went back into the flat and the old man switched off the mains again. I scrabbled in the darkness and slid the alarm off the ceiling, and when it stopped ringing he put the lights back on. As I jumped down off the chair to give the old man the alarm box, I saw him hunched forward with his hands on his knees. He seemed to be struggling for breath, but then he righted himself and smiled in relief.

'Do you want me to phone the housing for you tomorrow?'

'I can never get through.'

'I'll give them a ring.'

'I don't need them. I won't have a fire.'

'I know, mate. But you have to have them. Anyway, I'll feel guilty if you have one.'

'Okay, okay. Well, put a note through the door or something after.'

'Alright, mate. What's your name?'

'Mr King.'

'Alright, well, we can get some sleep now anyway. Bye.'

'Take care,' said the old man, slamming the door.

When I got in I felt good about helping, but knew I'd only bothered because I wanted some kip. I supposed everyone else could sleep now too.

A few days after the incident with the smoke alarms, I saw Mr King doubled over again, near the entrance to the flats. I walked over and asked him if he was okay, and when he nodded, I put my key fob to the door. We got in the lift together and neither of us said anything until we reached my floor, when Mr King told me he had something.

As we entered his flat, I was struck by the squalor, something I hadn't noticed before. I remembered the layout of the living room, with the armchair placed directly in front of the TV, but now I saw the dirty carpet and bruises of damp in two corners of the ceiling.

Mr King came out of the bedroom with an orange plastic

chair for me to sit on. Then he went to the kitchen and came back with an unopened bottle of whisky.

'You like whisky?' he asked.

'Yeah, I do.'

He twisted out the cork and poured some whisky into mugs. As we each took a sip, I leaned back in the chair.

In the corner there was a table with a broken leg. On top of it was a hexagon-shaped biscuit tin, with the lid balanced on top. Mr King saw me looking at it and told me to bring it over.

The box was full of cigarette cards, and Mr King shuffled through them before squinting at one in particular. The card was the size of the tiniest of mobile phones, and on the front was a painted picture of a man on a black motorbike. Smoke poured from a long exhaust and thin tyres threw back gravel. The rider hunched over a number 1 on the front, black goggles staring out from beneath a brown leather helmet. Behind him there was a green field, and in the top corner it said 'Will's Cigarettes'. In the bottom corner, just below the bike's back tyre, it said 'Senior T.T. Race 1930'.

I turned the card over and saw the name 'C.J.P. King' underlined on the back. Not yet putting two and two together, I took another sip of whisky before reading:

> Charles J.P. ('Charlie') King's sand and road racing successes on Sunbeam machines are almost legion. Sand racing at Southport and other Northern venues was, at first, his speciality, but it was his win in the 1929 Senior T.T. race that first made him famous. He also won the Belgian and German Grand Prix Races in that year. In 1930 King won both the French and Belgian Grand Prix, but he will always be remembered for his historic victory (at 72.05 m.p.h.) in the 1930 Senior Tourist Trophy Race, during which he broke the lap record no fewer than three times.

I looked up at Mr King, who sat there smiling. I turned the card over to look at the picture again, and when I said, 'Is this you, then?' he just nodded.

'1930, Jesus. You must be about a hundred years old.'

'Ninety-five.'

'It's no wonder you're a bit deaf.'

'What do you mean?'

'I said it—it doesn't matter. Ninety-five. Jesus. I'll drink to that,' I said.

'Do you mind if I call you Charlie?'

'Mr King.'

'Okay.'

As we drank our whisky, I stared out of the window and saw what looked like a parrot. Its feathers were as green as moss and when it moved nervously from branch to branch, I saw that its underside was bright yellow. I realized it was too small to be a parrot, and it certainly didn't sound like one, but I marvelled at it nonetheless.

I didn't want to overstay my welcome, so I thanked Mr King for the whisky and said it was time I left. He smiled, pointed at the cigarette cards, and said, 'They were all my friends, you know. All of them.'

Back in my flat, the first thing I did was switch on the TV, but there was nothing worth watching. When I got up the next morning I looked out of the window to see a man in a cherry picker taking the boards off the windows of the European Opera Centre. I was curious to know why, so I got dressed and went outside.

THE CRICKET BOOK SELLER

Warren Woodcock's home in Sussex was filled with cricket books of all kinds; biographies, autobiographies, tour diaries, scorebooks, rare and antiquarian books. He placed a regular advert in *The Cricketer*, and bought and sold second hand books via the mail.

≈

Chris Booth played cricket for a club in the Cheshire County league. Though only seventeen, he was a regular fixture in the 1st team, had a part time job on the ground staff at Old Trafford, and wanted to play for Lancashire.

When mates of his own age went out to pubs on a Friday, he cycled to the cricket club to practice for the game the following day. At night, he'd lie in bed reading cricket books and fall asleep to dream about playing for England.

His favourite book was called *Viv Richard's Cricket Masterclass*. It was full of advice on technique, as well as on the mental approach to the game. Viv Richards had been one of the greatest batsmen the world had ever seen, and since reading the book Chris had begun to score prolifically, imagining himself to be Richard's every time he walked out to bat.

The day after he scored his first century, Chris was sitting in the living room reading the latest issue of *The Cricketer*. His mum was out shopping and his dad was still in bed, so Chris sat reading quietly. Soon his dad got up and came downstairs, coughing. 'Get that kettle on,' he said, walking past the living room and into the kitchen.

Chris got up and Joe came in and sat drinking his tea where Chris had been sitting before. Then he put the TV on, lit a cigarette and started flicking through the channels.

'Can we watch the cricket?' said Chris.

'No. I'm not watching the cricket.'

'Oh . . .'

'Don't start moaning and groaning. You played cricket all day yesterday, didn't you? Do something else for a change.' Joe put on a taped Coronation Street and Chris settled back to read from his magazine. After a few minutes he looked up to see smoke stretching across the room.

From his bedroom Chris could see the slate roof and chimney of the house opposite, and telephone wires stretching like cracks across the window. A group of pigeons sat together near the chimney, and two of them kept sliding on the tiles as they tried to mate.

Looking at the row of cricket books on the windowsill, Chris imagined a day when he'd have so many books that he could fill a dozen shelves. On the next to last page of *The Cricketer*, he saw Warren Woodcock's advertisement, and decided to send for a catalogue.

~

The postman usually walked up the ramp to Warren's house with large piles of mail. The bulk of it was correspondence from fellow cricket book lovers. Sifting through the post, Warren tossed the junk mail aside and picked up a letter with a Manchester postmark:

Dear Warren,

As you know, the Old Trafford test match is coming up soon. I've got the tickets as usual, but I was wondering if you wanted to stay with us again this time? The reason I ask is that they've built a hotel right next to the ground, and I've heard that it's excellent, disabled access, room service etc. Not too expensive either.

You are more than welcome to stay with us again this time, but I just thought it might be easier for you. Anyway, let me know what you think.

Sincerely,
Alec Swanton.

Warren smiled. He'd been staying with Alec and his wife after the Old Trafford test match for the last five years. Since the accident, they'd been only too happy to have him stay with them, but the novelty had begun to fade like a pair of old jeans. Opening the remaining letters, Warren noticed among them Chris's request for a catalogue. He picked one up and placed it in an envelope.

∾

When Chris received the catalogue he saw the autobiographies of some great cricketers of the past: Gordon Greenidge, Michael Holding, Wasim Akram, Steve Waugh, Ian Botham, David Gower. One book in particular caught his eye: *The Art of Cricket* by Donald Bradman. It cost a fiver, and Chris immediately asked his mum to write a cheque.

'What's all this then?' said Joe.

'Well, he hasn't got his own cheque book, has he.'

'I hope he's giving you the money. We can't afford to buy old cricket books.'

'You don't even know what book it is,' said Chris.

'*The Art of Cricket* isn't it?'

'How do you know?'

'Well, you put a circle around it, didn't you? I'm not stupid you know. Why don't you get a book by an English player for a change? First it was West Indians, now it's Aussies. What do you want to buy an Aussie's book for?'

'He was the best batsman ever.'

'Yeah, well, it's too late to help you. What are you? Seventeen?

If you were going to play for Lancashire they would have snapped you up by now.'

'Leave him alone, Joe. There, I've written it.'

'If you're going to the post box you can get me an *Evening News* while you're out,' said Joe.

∼

When Warren got the cheque through, he noticed the phone number that Chris had put on the letter, and the next day gave him a ring.

'Hello?' answered Joe.

'Err, yes, hello. My name is Warren Woodcock. Can I speak to Christopher, please?'

'Err, yes. Hang on a minute.'

'Chris! Chris!'

'What?'

'Telephone!'

'Who is it?' he said, coming down the stairs.

'It's that cricket book bloke.'

'Hello?'

'Ah, hello Christopher. It's Warren Woodcock here, cricket book specialist.'

'Oh, alright?'

'Yes, yes, of course. I have your order here for *The Art of Cricket*, by Sir Donald Bradman.'

'Oh, right.'

'The thing is, I'm going to be in Manchester for the Old Trafford test match next week and I was wondering if perhaps we could meet. Do you have a ticket?'

'No, I don't, but . . . '

'Well, we could meet outside.'

'Well, no, I'll be working. I'm on the ground staff.'

'Oh well, even better. I'll be there on Friday, so I can bring your book along and we can meet. Do you have a mobile telephone number?'

'Err, yeah, just hang on.'

∼

Warren and Alec viewed the rain-interrupted day from the comfort of Warren's balcony. Sipping from a glass of white wine, Warren watched as the ground staff boys rushed on and off with the covers.

England had the better of the rain affected day, reducing the West Indies to 142 – 6 in the 42 overs possible. Warren had dinner with Alec in the pavilion suite and then made his way over to the club shop, where he'd arranged to meet Chris.

'I'd guessed that was you,' said Warren, as Chris appeared from around the corner.

'Mr Woodcock?'

'Warren, please.'

'Warren, sorry.'

'Did you have a good day?'

'Yeah, bit tired though.'

'I'm not surprised. How many times did the covers come on?'

'Oh, I don't know. I lost count.'

'Yes, I can imagine. Anyhow, I have your book, but I've left it in my room at the hotel. It's just over there though. Why don't we go and get it?'

'Err, yes, okay.'

The ground was littered with plastic pint pots and discarded signs with '4' on one side and '6' on the other. Steel shutters of a closed bar rippled in the wind as raindrops blurred chalk on a menu.

In the room Warren took off his jacket and threw it on the bed, then wheeled himself out onto the balcony. Beneath the giant scoreboard, an old man stamped a spade into the outfield as the sunset turned him pink.

'This is a wonderful view isn't it, Christopher?'

'Yeah, it's amazing.'

'I bet you would love to be out there playing, wouldn't you?'

'Yeah, I'd like to one day. My dad says I'm already too old to make it.'

'Oh, that's nonsense. How old are you?'

'Seventeen, nearly eighteen.'

'Seventeen? You have your whole life ahead of you. So much to discover.'

Chris looked around for the book as Warren began to pour

another glass of white wine. 'You'll join me, won't you? It's the least you deserve after running around in the rain all day. Come and sit over here,' said Warren.

Chris sat down on the bed and Warren passed him a glass of wine. As Chris took a sip, Warren put the TV on. 'Hey, that's good timing, we can watch the highlights,' said Warren, pointing to the screen.

'Err, I should be going soon. Have you got the book then?'

'Oh, yes, of course. I have it right here,' he said.

Chris looked lovingly at the book. It was in pristine condition, with a brown hardback cover and gold lettering on the spine. He flicked through to some black and white photographs showing Don Bradman in a mixture of action shots and fixed poses, depicting the forward defensive, the pull, the hook, the leg glance and the cover drive. Other pictures showed him bent over in the slips, or fielding in the covers, balanced like a figurine on the grass.

'Its in good condition isn't it,' said Warren.

'Yeah. It's great.'

'Look, there's the first wicket,' said Warren, pointing to the TV and watching as the West Indian opener fell to a sharply rising delivery.

'Oh, yeah.'

'Pass me your glass, would you?'

Chris drank what was left, then gave the glass to Warren, who re-filled it to the brim as the second wicket fell.

'That was a wonderful catch wasn't it, Christopher?'

'Yeah' said Chris, feeling his face begin to flush.

'He must have enormous hands. How big are yours? Show me your hands.'

Chris raised his right hand, and watched as Warren rested his own hand up against it.

'Your hands are much bigger than mine,' said Warren.

'Yeah,' said Chris, moving his hand away and looking back at the TV.

After an advertisement came on, Chris got up to go to the toilet, brushing against the side of the bed on his way out. Warren poured them both another glass of wine, and then rested his hands in his lap.

When Chris's mobile phone began to ring, Warren turned it off.

'The highlights are back on,' said Warren, as Chris came back in.

'Did I hear my phone?'

'Err, oh yes. I've got it here, you must have dropped it on the bed.'

'Missed call. My mum phoned.'

'Oh, right. I just switched it off. I didn't want to answer it.'

Chris picked the phone up and returned the call. 'Hi mum, did you ring?' he said.

'Yes. I did. Why did you turn your phone off?'

'I didn't.'

'Well I got cut off. Where are you? I was expecting you home by now.'

'Yeah, err, yeah, I'm just on my way.'

'Oh, alright then. I was just worried, that's all.'

'Okay. I'll get the tram. Won't be long.'

'Okay then, love. See you in a bit.'

'Yeah. See you in a bit.'

Chris put the phone in his pocket, before picking the book up off the bed.

'Here, have one more,' said Warren, holding out another glass.

'No. It's okay, I'm going to have to go.'

'What about the rest of the highlights?'

'I've got to go. My mum's worried,' said Chris, making his way to the door.

'Let me get the door,' said Warren, wheeling his way across the room.

'It's okay, I've got it,' said Chris.

'No wait, I'll get it,' said Warren, wheeling nearer.

'No really . . .' said Chris. 'I've got it.'

Warren's chair hit the inside of the door as Chris hurried away. Outside, the crowds had gone and Chris heard what sounded like a slowly fusing wire. Running as quickly as he could, he just made it to the tram stop in time.

He gazed from the window as the tram neared the centre of Manchester. Opposite him a woman sat with her cleavage presented like two plumped cushions. Chris continued to look from the window as the tram crossed over the Irwell towards Deansgate and, as the familiar vistas passed before his unseeing eyes, he thought about the touch of Warren's hand. Forgetting to get off at Oxford Road, he made his way out of Piccadilly Station and walked down Canal Street to the bus stop.

WAITING IN THE WINGS

Jack's daughter Heather was in a band, and he'd become their manager. For two years he booked time off work to drive them to gigs. Then the chance came to take voluntary redundancy and when the cheque cleared he bought himself a bottle of champagne.

Satori were well established in their hometown of Manchester and had been on a mini tour around the country, playing gigs in Leeds, Wolverhampton, Northampton, Liverpool and London. The final date of the tour was at the Bull and Gate in Camden Town.

On the morning of the gig, Jack went to Salford Van Hire for the mini-bus. Neal was picked up first and sat in the front—he was Heather's brother and came to help with the amps. Mark and Julian got in next, then Courtney and Heather.

Pulling out of the services near Birmingham, Neal watched a man in a luminous jacket picking up leaves from the grass. As the van accelerated away, Mark leaned over and prodded Neal with an REM tape.

'God, I thought Radiohead was depressing enough,' said Jack.

'Yeah? I don't mind,' said Neal.

Soon everyone fell asleep and Jack turned the music down. Glancing occasionally at his A-Z, he kept a steady speed in the middle lane of the motorway.

Neal woke up as the van passed through Highgate, rubbing his eyes then wiping condensation from the window. When the van stopped in Camden, everyone else started to move about. Jack parked the van around the corner from the Bull and Gate and they unloaded the gear.

There were four big amplifiers, a keyboard, six guitars and the drum kit. Neal and Jack carried the amps, Julian struggled with his drum kit and the rest of them got the guitars. When all the gear had been brought in through the fire exit, Neal and Jack went into the bar as the band set things up on stage.

'Found it easy enough then, Jack,' said Neal.

'Yeah, even though my A-Z man fell asleep.'

'Ha. Sorry about that, mate.'

'No, you're alright Neal, I'm only kidding.'

'I'll get you a drink anyway. Pint?'

'No, I'd better not. Just make it a coke.'

'Last one, eh?' said Neal, when he got back.

'Yeah, don't know what I'm going to do with myself.'

'At least you won't miss many more City games.'

'That's true. Mind you, I'm sure Heather will sort out more gigs.'

'Be good if someone came tonight, wouldn't it?'

'Well, yeah. This is supposed to be a really good place. They reckon Led Zep played here once.'

'Oh, yeah?'

'Courtney reckons there might be some record company people here tonight too. That's why they're all nervous, or more nervous than usual anyway.'

'Best to keep clear before the gig.'

'And after. You remember what they were like after Wolverhampton.'

At the sound check each member of the band played their instrument and looked anxiously towards Neal and Jack, who'd come back in to give the thumbs-up.

'I don't know what they worry about. They always sound great,' said Jack.

'Yeah. I think Mark said they can never hear themselves when they're on stage. It's because the amps are pointing this way and they haven't got monitors.'

'Oh, right.'

The promoter said they'd be filming the gig, and the band was excited by the prospect. A copy of the video was available for twenty quid, and Jack had the money.

The two bands on before Satori were local favourites and went down well with the gang of friends and family who'd come to watch. As Satori emerged on to the stage, Neal and Jack moved to the front.

After a mumbled introduction, the band started the set. Neal and Jack were as animated as their natures allowed, nodding their heads in time to the familiar tunes. As he applauded, Neal realized that his enthusiasm had turned into loyalty. This must have been about the twentieth time he'd seen Satori, and the fifth time he'd seen the same set.

Jack's hands were always the first to come together at the end of a gig, but the response overall was quieter than the band had become accustomed to. As the evening wore on they sold a few CDs, and Neal and Jack reassured them of how good they'd been.

Jack picked up the video from the promoter as the band milled around talking and drinking. He scratched his head and bought another coke, leaning on and off the bar as he waited.

By one in the morning Neal and Jack had taken it upon themselves to load up the gear. After they'd finished, they sat together in the van, and when the windscreen began to clear, a man stood before them in a yellow suit, picking up rubbish with a shiny metal stick.

'I wouldn't fancy that, Jack.'

'No, me neither. Mind you, he's probably getting a decent whack for working at this time.'

'Yeah . . . where was it you used to work anyway?'

'Astra Zeneca, in Carrington.'

'Near the United place?'

'Yeah.'

'So what was the job?'

'In the end I was doing health and safety stuff, regulations and all that.'

'That health and safety stuff is mad these days, isn't it?'

'True, Neal. In the old days nobody bothered,' said Jack, showing Neal a stump where his right thumb had been.

'Yeah, I was wondering how that happened.'

'Could have been a pianist you know,' he said, smiling.

'Ha, yeah right, leave that to Heather, mate. No, but really, how did it happen?'

'It was a forklift truck did it. No guard. I had my hand on it and the driver started lifting something up. My hand got stuck and it sliced the old Tom off, blood everywhere.'

'Couldn't they sow it back on?'

'No, that bloody driver panicked and went over it, reversed back, and went over it again. By the time he was finished it wouldn't have even bunged up a sink. Still, I get twenty quid a week for the rest of my life.'

'Twenty quid a week, eh?'

'Yeah, weird though, I'd rather have it back. You know what I mean?'

'Yeah.'

By the time the band made their way back to the van, the pavements were silver with frost, and the moon was as clear as an airbrushed eyeball.

'Are you stopping at the same services?' said Heather.

'Yeah, I'll need another coffee,' said Jack.

'Don't go dropping off at the wheel, will you?' said Courtney.

'No, don't worry. You get your head down for a bit.'

'Yeah, we'll try.'

When the van stopped at the services, everyone but Julian got off and went to the toilet. It was four in the morning, and their breath whipped behind them as they crossed a car park full of lorries.

Inside the services the red lights from a fruit machine flickered across the buffed white floor, and when Neal came out of the toilets he heard the sound of pots being washed in the kitchen. Jack finished the coffee from his flask and when they were on the motorway again Neal drifted into sleep as white lines fired past the van.

Back in Manchester, Mark and Julian were dropped off first, then Heather and Courtney. Neal was last to get out because he lived just around the corner from Jack's house in Moss Side.

'Here you go, Neal,' said Jack, pulling up to the kerb.

'Cheers, Jack. You get some kip when you get in.'

'Oh don't worry about me, son.'

'Alright, Jack. Cheers, mate.'

'Cheers,' said Jack, as Neal slammed the door.

Earlier that morning the sky had been an untouched blue, but it was overcast by the time Neal felt for his keys.

∾

A few months after the Camden gig, Jack phoned Neal to tell him that the band had signed a deal with a small record label. He also said they'd be getting some proper roadies, and a new manager to help them to the next level.

Neal saw the debut album advertised in a Sunday supplement, and went into town for it the next day. He knew all the tracks on the album, but the studio production gave the tunes a polished feel he didn't like. Putting it to one side, he dug out a live recording from the early days and, cranking up the volume, wallowed in the ragged glory of the only time he'd ever felt part of something.

Jack invited him over one night so they could listen to the new album together. When Jack opened the champagne, Neal held out his glass and watched the bubbles overflow onto the carpet. In the silence at the end of the album, Jack sipped what was left of the champagne, and when he came back out of the kitchen with a cloth and started scrubbing the floor, Neal changed the music.

THE EMPTY SPACE

Mary got into the back of the minibus and sat with the others looking at the rain that ran down the windows. The grey morning had gradually brightened into a flat whiteness by the time they trailed into the factory.

Inside, the smell of soap filled the air as they put on their overalls. Mary wasn't really listening, but when a man with a pair of blue knickers over his beard pointed towards the far end of the factory, Mary followed a middle aged woman past different conveyor belts and loading bays. Walking at right angles around zones marked off by yellow paint, they moved towards the far end of the factory, where another woman stood perched on top of a silver ladder, unblocking the path of detergent bottles. When she got off the ladder she pointed to where Mary should stand, and when Mary moved there the conveyor was switched back on. Mary had to stand back a bit from the belt and felt a kick as the detergent bottles began to flow past her.

'Wakey, wakey!' shouted the woman, above the cranking rattle of the conveyor.

'What?' said Mary.

'Screw the tops on, love, don't just bloody stand there.'

'Oh, right,' said Mary.

On the table next to the conveyor there was a pile of white screw tops, and as the bottles dawdled past, Mary put the tops onto them. Two hours later, at nine, the woman told Mary that it was break time, and Mary followed her to the canteen.

In the windowless room Mary watched as people in blue overalls and red boots got cans of coke from the coke machine,
chocolate bars from the snack machine, and tea or coffee from
the hot drinks machine. Mary got herself a chocolate bar and a
cup of tea, and when she sat down at the end of a busy table she
sipped the soothing drink.

As she looked down the long white table, Mary saw people
reading newspapers or unwrapping the foil or cling film from
around sandwiches. She reached down beneath the table and
took her own food out of a carrier bag, and began to eat the
cheese sandwiches she'd made earlier in the morning.

After ten minutes, Mary walked back to the conveyor where
the woman from before waited beside the switch. Mary took up
her position and stretched her back before the slow procession
of bottles resumed. Standing there screwing on the bottle tops,
Mary thought about names.

At lunchtime Mary sat in a toilet cubicle and read the graffiti
on the walls. She closed her eyes and drifted away, and then
woke with a start to see that it was time to go back to work.

There were two and a half hours to do in the afternoon, and
there was a ten-minute break halfway through that. As she
screwed the bottle tops on, Mary thought of what she might
make for her tea. At three, she took off her overalls and waited
in the car park with the rest of the agency workers. As they sat
back in the minibus and moved down the slip road towards the
motorway, Mary listened to the mixture of languages, and
squinted through the window at the faces in passing cars.

After getting out of the minibus, Mary waited for the bus.
When she got on, she smiled at the people sitting in the chairs
at the front and then, when none of them got up, walked to a
free seat near the back.

~

It was night, it was always night, when he lay beside her, against
her. She loved him and was glad he was there beside her in the
dark, and then she wished he would go, stop it and go, go away
and leave her alone again in the dark, alone.

At breakfast she'd watch them together, happy, smiling,
caught up in the comfortable routines of the morning. He

kissed her on the cheek and then told them goodbye, and she'd go to school with the ache that lingered from before.

In school she'd stand by the railings at playtime and watch cars passing by on the road. In class she couldn't concentrate, often struggling to stay awake, but she liked it there because it was warm, and sometimes, when the teacher read stories, she felt far away.

At the end of the day, when all the other kids streamed home together, she would wait by the railings. When she eventually began to make her way home, she walked slowly through the quiet streets, sometimes stopping to stroke a cat on a wall, or a dog poking its nose through a gate.

Every day the lollipop man had to wait for her, and after he'd seen her across the road, he'd take off his hat and light a cigarette and drag his sign along the pavement behind them.

Approaching the house, she'd look at the empty space where the car would be, then go in through the front gate, lifting it on to its hinges to stop it from squeaking. Once inside, she'd get a chocolate bar and a cup of tea, and sit watching cartoons with her mum and the twins. Then, when she heard the car pulling up outside the house, she'd go upstairs and watch the TV in her bedroom.

Years later, in the court, he'd lied about it all, and her sisters said nothing, even though she'd heard him going into their room. The family asked her over and over why she was doing this to them, and when he was cleared, they never spoke to her again.

～

Not long after the baby was born, Mary began working as a barmaid. With Karolyn in her pram just by the till, Mary served the trickle of daytime punters. Sitting on a stool by the end of the bar she smoked cigarettes and drank tea, watching as various men played the fruit machines, or read from newspapers, or watched the sport on TV. At half five, Kevin came in, rested his hard hat on the bar and unfastened his luminous waistcoat.

'Alright, love, how's the sprog?'

'She's alright. What do you care anyway?'

'Shut up and get me a Stella.'

Mary poured his pint, and then came out from behind the bar and sat on a stool next to him, tickling the back of his neck with her fingernails. He kissed her on the cheek and then turned away from her to watch the cricket on TV. She lit another cigarette and jumped off the stool when Dave smiled his sad smile.

When Janet came in, Mary wheeled the pram out from behind the bar. She sat on the stool next to Kevin, the baby between them, and ate a chocolate bar. When Kevin got another drink he bought Mary a half and she sat there drinking and smoking while he watched TV.

Just after eight, Kevin got off his stool and they left, saying goodbye to Janet before dropping in to the chippy on the way home. When they got in, Mary put the chips onto plates, and buttered some bread for Kevin. She took it in to him on a tray, and when he asked for a lager she went back into the kitchen and came back out with a can. As he sat eating his chips in front of the TV, Mary put Karolyn to bed and came back downstairs to sit beside Kevin on the couch. When he finished his chips he got the biscuit tin out from under the couch and rolled a joint that they smoked together before shuffling upstairs to bed.

Mary lay there with her eyes closed as Kevin pushed gently inside her. When he rolled off he kissed her on the cheek, and within minutes was fast asleep. Mary lay there in the dark, then pulled up her knickers and got out of bed. She cleaned herself beneath the harsh white light of the bathroom, and checked on Karolyn before walking back into the bedroom and setting the alarm on Kevin's side of the bed. Climbing under the covers, she looked over at the window. A tiny gap in the curtains sent a line of white light across the bed, and Mary fell asleep as the lights of cars passed across the ceiling above her.

THE ROOMS

Inger Molby was a Danish installation artist and called her latest project *The Rooms*. She'd been to New York and Berlin to take photographs of apartments, and with the rest of her grant from the Danish Arts Council she decided to go to Manchester.

Jenny Aldred was an art student at Manchester Metropolitan University, and had recently split up with her boyfriend. She kept busy all the time; painting, drawing, sculpting, writing poetry or playing her guitar. When she saw Inger's advert she decided to apply, and soon afterwards they met.

In a coffee shop opposite the BBC building on Oxford Road, they introduced themselves to one another and Inger showed Jenny the following quotation:

> To begin with the question concerning external existence, it may perhaps be said, that ... our own body evidently belongs to us; and as several impressions appear exterior to the body ... The paper, on which I write at present, is beyond my hand. The table is beyond the paper. The walls of the chamber beyond the table. And in casting my eye towards the window, I perceive a great extent of fields and buildings beyond my chamber. From all this it may be infer'd, that no other faculty is requir'd, beside the senses, to convince us of the external existence of body.
> —DAVID HUME: *A Treatise of Human Nature*

Jenny agreed to join the project, despite the fact that she'd be working as an unpaid labourer, carting Inger's photography equipment from flat to flat.

As Inger had yet to decide on where to take the pictures, she welcomed Jenny's suggestions. They tried to get permission to photograph in some loft apartments on Deansgate, but there was too much hassle involved in arranging access and making appointments with the residents.

When Inger went back to Jenny's for coffee after spending a frustrating day wandering around town, she welcomed the suggestion to do the project in Jenny's building.

Lambeth Court was a council block built in the sixties, containing eighty identically sized flats. After sharing a bottle of wine, Inger and Jenny agreed to start the following morning.

Jenny got up early, drinking tea and strumming her guitar while she waited for Inger to arrive. Inger was an hour late, but Jenny didn't mind as she'd composed a melody in the meantime.

'Am I late? My husband didn't wake me up on time in the hotel. He's useless,' said Inger, resting her photography equipment on Jenny's floor.

'It's okay.'

'Are you ready to make a start?'

'Err, yes. There's a lot of stuff.'

'Do you think so? It's the lighting. We have to get the lighting correct. Look at the camera, it's not too big, amazing really. Here,' said Inger, passing Jenny the large tripod for the light, then two shoulder bags, one with various films and filters, and another one containing the light itself.

As Jenny lived on the eighth floor it was logical to work from the top down, so first of all they knocked on the doors of Jenny's closest neighbours. Nobody answered, and Jenny began to ponder the wisdom of doing the project in midweek.

On the seventh floor a young man called Anthony opened his door and welcomed them in. An artist himself, he was intrigued. Jenny compared her own flat to his and admired what he'd done with the space. The living room was almost entirely white; white painted floorboards, white walls, white ceiling, white blinds on the windows. The only furniture was a single settee, covered in a lacy white throw, and a small circular table with a cup and saucer on it.

'Oh, I love what you've done with your apartment,' said Inger.

'Well, thanks, honey. I do my best, you know. One needs to live to a comfortable standard,' he said, laughing.

'Ha, ha,' laughed Inger.

'Can I make you a cup of tea, my darlings?' he said.

'Yes, okay,' said Inger.

As Inger and Anthony talked about their art, Jenny sat on the other end of the settee, picturing her ex-boyfriend in his boxer shorts, playing a guitar.

After two cups of tea, Inger eventually decided it was time to take the pictures. She positioned the camera as far back from the windows as possible, and then showed Jenny how to set up the tripod and affix the light. Inger looked down into her camera, which also sat on a tripod, and made various tiny adjustments.

Anthony hovered around, asking Inger about the camera. Soon enough the pictures were taken, and Anthony gave them the numbers of two friends who also lived in the building.

The next flat they went into was owned by a young woman called Nicky; an edgy, attractive young woman with dread-locked black hair. Her living room was full of guitars, and Jenny counted seven in all—four electric and three acoustic. As well as the guitars, there was a banjo on the couch and a trumpet on the table. The walls were lined with black and white prints of rock stars. There were no blinds on the windows, and the three square panes each had a wind chime dangling above.

Jenny and Inger set up the tripods, lighting and camera. Nicky began to tidy a sliding pile of magazines, but Inger barked at her to leave them as they were. She reminded Nicky that it was essential to the project that things should look as natural as possible, the differences within the templates of each room reflecting the taste and lifestyle of the occupant.

In the next flat along, a middle-aged woman called Sandra opened the door to them. When Inger looked down into the camera, the square was taken up by a circular dining table covered in an orange brocaded cloth, surrounded by the shoulders of four mahogany chairs. In the middle of the table there was a glass bowl of oranges, and above it, a golden lampshade. Beyond the table, the windowsill was covered in pink and blue flowers, the smell of which filled the room. The windows themselves were sparklingly clear and seemed to add definition to the trees outside. On one side of the window there hung a black and white photograph of a cathedral, and on the other an ornate clock with motionless gold hands.

It had taken them all day to take photographs of three flats, and at five in the evening Inger told Jenny she'd had enough and would be back at nine the following day.

In the morning Inger and Jenny knocked on door after door, and nobody answered, though sometimes they saw movements of light through the keyhole. Finally, on the third floor, a tall man with a red beard showed them in.

In Andy's living room, white light struggled in through the dirty blinds. A black tiled floor had a footpath through dust leading to the couch where he sat, drinking from a can of beer. Two squashed empties leaned against the couch by his feet, and the clock on the video said half past eleven.

'I'm not sure it's going to be light enough in here,' said Inger.

'Really?' Jenny answered.

'No. I don't think so.'

'Well, at least let's give it a try. Let me set the light up.'

'Okay, then,' said Inger.

'Hey, do you want me to get out of your way?' said Andy.

'Erm. Not yet. But I'll need you to move in a few minutes.'

'Alright,' he said, standing up.

'No! Not yet. In a few minutes, I said.'

'Oh, alright. Sorry.'

Jenny had already got the lighting ready and glanced around the room as she waited for Inger. A stereo system rested against the wall and the cassette door leaned open like a broken purse. Inger told Andy to move out of shot and proceeded to take the pictures.

'Like I told you, Jenny, I don't think these are going to come out very well, and I'm not sure it's what we want,' Inger said.

'Well, we'll see. It doesn't matter if they are a bit darker, does it?'

When they finished Andy offered them a beer, but they declined.

'Wow. It was pretty rough in there, wasn't it?' said Inger, on the stairs.

'It wasn't that bad, come on. I know it isn't New York, or Berlin, but I'm sure everyone doesn't live in luxury there either.'

'I'm not sure we should try any more. They look pretty rough.'

'Oh, come on. Is it just pretty flats you want?'

'I'm not sure. I don't think these flats are going to look too good in my portfolio.'

'Well, what's the point of just filming the nice ones?'

'I'm not sure what the project is about any more.'

'What do you mean?'

'Well, to be honest, it's becoming less clear in my head, the more rooms I take pictures of.'

'Is it because you don't want to take pictures of poor people?'

'No, it's not that.'

'Right,' said Jenny.

'Okay, okay. I suppose there's time for one more, but then I need to get back to the hotel to pack.'

'Pack?'

'Yeah, we're going back tomorrow. We need to spend some time away from each other.'

On the first floor, a man with a skinhead brushed past them on his way to the lift. Inger stared after him, and Jenny knocked on a door.

'Yeah?' a hassled looking woman said.

'Hi. I'm doing a project, taking pictures of people's flats. Could we come in?' said Inger.

'What?'

'Could we come in and take some pictures?'

'What? Of my flat? Why?'

'Well, I post a picture to everyone that I photograph.'

'Why would I want a picture of my own flat, love?'

'Okay. It doesn't matter. We'll try someone else.'

'I wouldn't bother on this floor, love. None of them will be up yet.'

'Okay, well, we'll try for ourselves.'

'Hey, don't take that tone with me, love.'

'What tone?'

'You know what I mean.'

'What?'

'You heard me, you posh foreign bitch,' she said, stepping out of her doorway.

'What are you doing?'' said Inger, as the woman approached.

'Fuck off, you bitch.'

'Okay, Jenny, let's go.'

'Hey, where do you think you're going?'

'It's okay, we're going,' said Jenny.

'You keep your fucking nose out too,' she said, pushing Inger.

Inger shoved back and the woman stumbled. As a couple of kids emerged from the living room to ask their mummy what was wrong, mummy ran at Inger. Jenny took out her mobile, and missed the sight of Inger's legs flipping over the rail.

Jenny gazed down at the body that lay star-shaped on the car park floor. Though Inger was quite obviously dead, she still seemed to be looking up, her open eyes fixed on a single blotch of cloud in the sky.

BETWEEN THE ZIPPED LIMITS

I'm sitting among the cold rocks of Swirral Edge, looking at Red Tarn through the mist as it disappears and re-appears again at the caprice of the wind. A fat crow flies past with a glow of orange peel in its black mouth, the slowly threshing wings like scissors cutting the air.

I came here on my own because I need a break from the relationship I'm in. While my girlfriend is at home, I'm watching hikers crawling around Red Tarn like ants skirting a puddle.

On the summit of Helvellyn a group of boys wearing matching fleeces frowned at me when I asked them for directions. They gave me a compass bearing and I laughed and wandered off through the mist, following cairns that looked like gremlins in the gloom. When the mist cleared I could see the path stretching down below, like white cotton thread on a dropped green sweater.

The whisky from my hip flask warms me, the uncorked malt clothing my throat like a scarf. The fat crow lands with a hush of wings and I pass it a piece of Mars bar.

≈

I met Paola outside a student pub in the quiet months of summer. She was talking in Spanish to her friend, and I walked over to listen to their voices. When we spoke it turned out we were both artists. She came from Madrid. I'd just started my own art magazine and was looking for submissions, so she invited me back to her flat.

The portfolio was full of interesting images — collages of lottery and raffle tickets over black and white photographs of historic buildings, a naked man in a cage, a silver ball in a corridor, a painting of a mouse with a tree growing out of its belly.

I looked with interest at the images, but soon became preoccupied with Paola's dark brown eyes and black hair, and the way her jeans curved in a tiny c around the small of her light brown back.

We've been together for about a year. I don't think I'm in love with her. When she said she was in love with me I was shocked. I felt the fear of a bad swimmer grasping for the surface, a sickening ache in my stomach located somewhere between tension and sorrow. I couldn't remember anyone else saying that to me. When Paola asked me if I loved her I said that I wasn't sure. She became upset, but I didn't want the relationship to end, so a day or so later I told her that I loved her.

~

Striding Edge is the most breathtaking mountain ridge in the Lake District. One stumble could mean crashing down for thousands of feet on either side of its slippery skyscraper ledge. From Patterdale, an easy walk gradually inclines its way into the Grisedale valley. Then it's a safe but steep ascent up a rocky track to a grassy plateau, where the timid walker can enjoy a sandwich and a flask of coffee while looking at the glistening black pond of Red Tarn, bobbing and sloshing beneath the ragged peaks above.

I was excited as I made my way across Striding Edge, my heart rate increased as I clung to rocks in the shoving wind and slipped on icy ground in my trainers. My ears stung pink in the ripping air and my hands were swollen with cold and bleeding on grappled-for stone. I felt my bare knees ache and my wet feet sliding inside my lumpy wet socks.

The ridge seemed to recede like melting ice beneath my feet, and the sun came in and out like car lights through a garden fence. My shaking legs and fear-filled chest made my scrambling slow, and the silent voids beside me beckoned like the ghosts waiting around the memorial on the mountain's peak.

Tutting hikers, sensibly clothed and wheezing in the breeze, pass me on their way down. As I start descending, the crow floats effortlessly back up to the sky. On the other rim of the circle around Red Tarn, a hesitant procession of black dots moves across Striding Edge. White light flashes like a memory through the clouds.

I start running down the mountain, jumping from rock to rock and taking to the air before a slip slides in. I brush past raincoats and woolly hats and leather boots and gloves and scarves and balaclavas and arctic mittens and ski sticks and walking sticks and compasses and maps and flasks and flapjacks and rucksacks. I look back up at them from a stone seat by the tarn, and think too long about going for a swim.

Descending into the Grisedale valley, I see a farmhouse with smoke curling from its chimney. I sip from my hip flask and speed up beneath the enclosing clouds.

Back in my cheap tent at the campsite on the farm in Patterdale, I look up from between the zipped limits at the clouds sliding like a black avalanche and hooding the peaks with water. A jet plane simulates thunder. Resolute midges nip at my face and I zip up the door. In the airless enclosure I think of Paola as rain plays on the tent roof like a thousand-fingered pianist.

I feel myself hardening beneath the musty cover of my torn and faded sleeping bag. The tent begins to leak and I lie there with droplets tapping on my shoulder. I can feel Paola's hair, and her skin beneath my hands.

I remember how we slept together a few times before we actually made love. One night, emerging from sleep to see the shadows of a tree across her naked back in the moonlight, I began to kiss her. We kissed for hours and hours before she gently moved on top of me. It was really slow at first, warm and wet and not uncomfortable like before.

After two nights camping at the farmhouse I pack up my tent and begin hiking back to Grasmere. At Grisedale Tarn white boats of light sink into the black water.

In a pub in Grasmere I get frowned at by a barman and told that the hikers bar is round the back. As I turn to leave I see silent couples hunched over meals, their cutlery flashing on the walls as the white light through the double glazed windows is scratched by silent rain.

I sit on a bench outside and remember the meals I've had with Paola, the things we made together that she described as 'Spanish omelette' or 'Spanish chicken', her English not able to be more specific, and how this language barrier led in other ways to rows.

The bus back to Windermere passes Wordsworth's Lodge, where Japanese tourists make films with tiny mobile phones, and old people in matching clothes walk around eating scones and drinking from delicate cups of tea. I see an old couple arguing with each other and the man waving a flashing stick in the direction of the lake, where a white motorboat whizzes past the eye like a blade.

The old green bus I'm on twirls around the winding road skirting the lake. A dribbling can of beer rolls from side to side, leaving golden trails on the floor. A tiny Chinese tourist sits on the seat before me, toying with a mobile phone.

I think of Paola and all the text messages I used to send to her, disguising my ignorance of Spanish by quoting from a bilingual edition of the poems of Pablo Neruda. *Tu Encendiste la vida*, meaning 'You set fire to life' was the first Spanish text that I sent to her. Another was the last line from Neruda's poem, 'Every Day You Play'. *Quiero hacer contigo lo que la primavera hace con los cerezos,* — 'I want to do with you what spring does to the cherry trees.' I remember how Paola responded to these, and how they must have seemed to her like missives of love.

At this memory her eyes and hair return, dark things of beauty in the white shining world, and I try to convince myself that I love her. But everything seems blurred by the difficulty of communication, the too palpable differences in the languages of our birth.

I recall the words of the poem I wrote about waking up with Paola, the one she didn't like:

Hangover Music

The green man
only guides ghosts

on mornings like these
and cranes turn
away from the horizon.

Nails on my throat
make mute birds sing
and the lacklustre
foot soldier awakes.

On the train back to Manchester, a couple of young Japanese women get me to take their picture by simply smiling and passing their phone camera. They laugh as I bumble with the technology, but the picture is taken. I watch as they replace their headphones and sit down opposite each other, their gazing faces twinned in the window's reflection.

The train passes by the back gardens of houses. On this sunny afternoon, I see old couples sitting on deck chairs angled perfectly into the heat, young children in a tiny paddling pool laughing as a fat father dips a toe in and stumbles away, a limping black dog being followed around a lawn by a flopping rabbit, an Asian man in loose white clothes kicking a football, girls doing handstands, cats in the shade, birds on a table, trees in the breeze.

I see a school playground, smoking cliques in corners, whirling bags and kicking feet. I hear the muffled noise of screaming and whistles. On the other side of the school a lone man marks out a rugby pitch, sunlight bouncing off his balding head as a trail of blackbirds watch from a new-painted crossbar.

From the track's elevation I see him depart from the straight line. He stops, scratches his head and looks at the slant that curls like a corner kerb towards the infield. I crane my neck round to see what he does next, and in my last glimpse from the train I'm sure I see him painting circles on the grass, the mountains of the Lake District shrinking like the pink reflections of the afternoon.

CLIMBING

At the top of the Devil's Staircase, Carol and Peter sat facing Buachaille Etive Mor, the giant herdsman of the glen that looked down on the myriad silver bloodshots of sky-lit tributaries and pools on Rannoch Moor.

After eating their sandwiches they descended the bedspring curves of the path, Peter following Carol in a twisting and turning run that was better for their knees than merely walking, and soon they reached the roadside. Waiting for a gap between coaches and cars they crossed over to the tiny white croft at the base of the mountain, gazing back at the staircase from a wooden bench in memory of a dead climber. The stream they'd skirted on their descent disappeared under the road and reappeared in a slow curl past the cottage, the white light shattered by rocks beneath a shifting haze of midges.

The croft behind them was a mountain rescue hut, and as they moved away and began the return up the valley to the Kingshouse, they could just make out the tiny pinheads of helmeted climbers on the mountainside, the thin hair of rope between them the only insurance against a life-taking fall.

Back at the campground behind the pub, they put their rucksacks in the tent and sat by the stream, the sweat on their bodies from the hike slowly cooling as they boiled water for tea. Drinking from the plastic mugs they watched clouds move down the valley and sprawl across the mountain's ridge for a time until the sun seemed to bump them away.

After getting changed they went into the pub, ordered a meal and sat drinking at a table beneath black and white photographs of climbers on the wall.

'I hope these are clean,' said Carol, picking up her knife and fork.

'Don't be paranoid,' whispered Peter.

'Don't call me paranoid,' said Carol.

Through the window they looked at the mountain that filled the oblong of glass like a watercolour. Beneath it, along the road, coaches and cars disappeared down the valley to Glencoe.

'That looks nice,' said Carol to Peter, as the barmaid put the food on the table.

'Yeah, so does yours,' said Peter.

'Thank you,' said Carol, to the barmaid.

'Yes, thank you,' said Peter.

Walking out of the pub and into the blackness lit only by the moon and stars, their eyes adjusted in time to make brief contact with the wired eyes of the head of a group of red deer. There were about a dozen of them, moving serenely across the valley, their hooves scraping on rock and dancing over grass before splashing through the moonlit stream.

Back in the tent, Carol put on her head torch and began reading, while Peter lay on his back listening to the water moving outside and struggling to free his mind from the memories that assailed him every night. When Carol put her book down and switched off the head torch, she kissed Peter on the cheek and turned away from him and onto her side, and Peter lay there with his eyes open, the only light coming from the whiteness of the moon gradually seeping through the fabric of the walls around them. In the silence broken only by the gentle brushing over rocks of the stream, Peter recognized once more the exact moment that always left him feeling briefly bereft and totally alone.

The christening had been held in the function room of the rugby club and was a raucous, packed affair. Beneath balloons and bunting, three lots of eleven rugby players, as well as their wives and partners and all the other invited guests, drank and raided the buffet and then danced and drank some more.

Carol sat in the corner with baby Shelley, alongside her mum and Peter's dad, while Peter moved around the room, accepting the offers of drinks and chatting to the people who bought them. All evening people came up to Carol and the baby, some-times kissing one or both of them before putting presents or cards on the growing pile beside. Peter made a short speech, during which he was playfully heckled by team-mates insensate with booze, but generally he felt roused and lifted inside by the warmth and well-wishes of people who'd seen him move from the junior's to the first X1.

Late in the evening, exhausted, he sat with Carol and Shelley and looked at himself as a teenager in a team photo on the wall. Then he smiled at Carol, tired but glowing as she held a sleeping Shelley to the soft wall of her breasts, and saw how the pain of the birth had transmuted itself into a loving interdependence, their beautiful baby completing the family they'd not even been sure they'd wanted.

Peter watched as his dad and Carol's mum danced together. Beside them was Arnold, the groundsman at the club, doing a kind of dyslexic version of the YMCA, a sight made more won-derful by the fact that he was usually the most cantankerous of men, a man soured rather than consoled by the solitude of a morning mow. Arnold's long-suffering wife Edna lay under the buffet table in the corner, her long dress bunched around her thighs after she'd slumped blissfully drunk onto the floor, large-ly ignored by friends familiar with her full use of any licence to let herself go.

Needing to use the toilet, Peter found it busy and so wan-dered to the dressing room, where he saw the bobbing backside of the young 1st X1 winger, rattling all hell out of a table with the help of a catering girl. Desperate, he walked past them to the cubicle, but they didn't seem to notice him, and when he went out the other way, through the car park and back round to the function room, he heard the table collapse and only a brief pause for laughter before the grunting and requests recom-menced with an even more intense vigour than before.

As he looked through the window of the function room, Peter saw the gold of the rising sun filtering across the rugby field, glinting on the tall H of the posts and on the rings and watches and scattered empty beer cans of the handful of juniors sitting on the summer grass. He thought of how he'd been that young not so long before, and had a brief sense of fondness for a freedom he'd once been so afraid of losing. He knew that in his years of playing for the club he must have stood on every inch of the field, and the minor triumphs and tragedies of cup runs and league campaigns were now made to seem almost insignificant by the realization of fatherhood; a fatherhood that felt not so much like a consolation for failed ambition, but a higher satisfaction to be gleaned only in the rosy aftermath of its fulfilment.

In the tent, Carol began to boil a pan of water for tea, and when Peter emerged from the coveted oblivious hours, she passed him his plastic mug from which he drank while still blinking into the light. She told him that she was no longer satisfied with just the view and wanted to climb Buachaille Etive Mor. He was initially surprised, but when, with some anticipation, he unzipped the tent doors to see the contours of the peak sharply outlined by the sunlit day, he too felt like climbing.

Judging from the map, it seemed like there was a pretty obvious path leading to the summit, and soon they were passing the rescue hut. At first the incline was pretty gradual and yet Peter soon began to feel himself breathing heavily. Determined not to ask Carol to stop, he no longer looked down at the view that broadened with every step and instead simply focussed on the back of Carol's boots, the rising and falling heels flicking back gravel from a sun-dusted path that subtly dampened and darkened with altitude.

Eventually Carol stopped by the side of the path, dropped the rucksack and took out a bottle of water that she opened and passed to Peter. Invigorated by the water and the rest they moved higher and higher, the path slowly obliterating into scree that moved the ground beneath their feet and slowed their progress to the lip of the ridge. There was a brief shower of cooling rain from a solitary drifting cloud in the sky, and soon they had to move on all fours, requiring the added purchase of their hands to reach the solid boulders higher.

From the peak they gazed down at the tiny white model of the Kingshouse, the road leading like a wire past the glittered heather on Rannoch Moor.

'Take a good look, Peter, and try to remember it.'

'I am.'

'You can see the car next to the pub.'

'Oh, yeah.'

'We'll come again.'

'Will we?'

'Of course we will.'

'I wish . . .'

'I know. Don't say it. It's okay.'

As they hugged, a white tailed eagle landed silently beside them, its talons clinging to a rocky outcrop. Carol and Peter could almost hear its breathing and, although each would be forever slowed by the aching irony of their baby being taken by a kiss, they would always remember the day they felt the full benevolence of the giant herdsman of the glen.

ACKNOWLEDGEMENTS

Acknowledgement is due to the editors of *Parameter Magazine*, where the story 'All Smiles Saved' first appeared.

The author would like to express his thanks to Andrew Biswell and Michael Schmidt.

Lightning Source UK Ltd.
Milton Keynes UK
18 July 2010

157173UK00001B/16/A